A Cold Night in

Rob Lofthouse

'Had you have known our boy, you would of loved him too.'
-Rudyard Kipling

Contents

Mention in Dispatches	7
PROLOGUE	11
1	13
2	22
3	36
4	49
5	59
6	68
7	79
8	88
9	94
10	109
11	121
12	126
13	132
14	142
15	152
EPILOGUE	160
Mount Longdon	168

Foreword by Major Justin Featherstone MC.

The Falklands Conflict was remarkable in many ways. It was the last British conflict over an issue of national sovereignty; the last significant British maritime military deployment; the last time that British troops marched for the duration of a campaign; the last time a substantial British task force met a regular enemy without any meaningful air manoeuvrability. This was primarily a dismounted infantry campaign, its battles fought in close combat, in a manner that has changed little since World War II.

One thing that has not altered lies at the very heart of British military capability, the British private soldier. As we accompany Archie and B Company of 3rd Battalion, The Parachute Regiment across the desolate and arduous terrain of the Falklands, Rob's treatment of the workings of such a force is both affecting and unerringly accurate. From preparation, to the orders given over a topological model constructed from earth, each episode drew me back to when I was giving orders for battle.

When Archie enters the maelstrom of close combat, the ordered chaos, sensory overload and sense of unyielding commitment are both overwhelming and compelling. The author conveys the horror and sense of movement without flinching, but it is the extraordinary actions of each individual which have the greatest impact.

As the battle progresses, and the cost mounts, the strength of initiative given to the ranks is apparent. It is this thoroughly British concept of Mission Command that allows 3 Para the flexibility and momentum to push home the attack, despite devastating losses. As each of the individuals constantly consider what they should do next in the absence of regular orders, having lost many of their commanders, they act with authority and a savage pride that ultimately leads to the defeat of the Argentine position on that remote 600-foot hill, despite the enemy's strength and the need to attack up the slope.

Rob has created a compassionate, emotive and compelling story, clearly born from the author's experiences as a combat infantryman. I remain honoured to have served in the field with many identifiable Archies and his authentic voice has remained with me long after I finished reading this story and that of 5 Platoon, B Company, 3 Para, and its desperate advance up the rock-strewn slopes of Mount Longdon.

Mention in Dispatches

'A Cold Night in June' started out as a vivid dream, and the following people helped me make it a reality...

My lovely wife, Vicky, and my three beautiful children, who for eighteen months put up with grunts and one word answers as I typed away, my two finger typing providing some amusement throughout.

Shaun & Nicky Langrish, family friends, who actually became the first fans of my work.

Justin Featherstone, Matt Maer and Danny Mills for giving me the time of day with the whole project.

Dan & Natalia Henwood, for their Argentine connections.

The team at 'The Argentina Independent' based in Buenos Aires. They provided me with the actual Argentine casualty list with features at the back of the book.

Major Manny Manfred. Manny was very complimentary about the book when he read it. Manny served as a Platoon Sergeant during the battle. He felt the book had been written by someone that was on the mountain that night back in June 1982. The fact being at the time of the battle, I was five years old.

Last by no means least, my agent Steve, who is sadly no longer with us. I owe Steve a debt I will never be able to repay, as it is with his guidance has put me where I am in the writing world.

Thank you, Steve.

This story, be it fiction is dedicated to the British and Argentine families of those who fell on that dreadful night, 35 years ago.

Mount Longdon 11th-12th June 1982

PROLOGUE

We got up mob handed, and dashed forward, grabbing the gun by the carry handle, I legged it to the first cluster of rocks I could hide behind. Just as the light faded from one flare, another took its place, we were so caught in the open, and we had to get in amongst the rocks. Jamie was right on my tail as we slid in behind some decent cover. I tried to site the gun in a decent position with the legs down, but I was too exposed, as tracer smashed into our cover. Legs up, lower profile. As I tried to get into position, our rocks would get hit with incoming fire. Jamie would lean out to his left and snap off a few shots with his SLR, but would then duck back in just as rounds would smash into our cover again. Pinned down here. As another flare lit up our position, I could see all order of formation had gone out of the window, the guys were literally behind cover in various sized groups just trying to get the upper hand. We had a fair idea which muzzle flash above us was giving us trouble, and some of the lads were giving it back as I could see red tracer splashing all over that position, and for a little while that position would be silent, but would start up again, maybe with a new gunner.

The din around us was tremendous, machine gun fire, screaming, shouting, you name it. I took the barrel bag off as the strap was really chaffing my neck. Jamie then grabbed my arm and pointed to the left. I could make out John shouting at me, but amongst the noise, I couldn't make out what he wanted. It became apparent, when everyone dashed out of cover and took a bound forward, I quickly grabbed the gun as Jamie already began sprinting forward. As I legged it after him, I noticed him jump over a small group of rocks, as I got close, green and orange tracer began to thud and smash into the ground just right of me, I changed direction and went for the rocks Jamie hurdled. I then tripped, and got a face full of timber and peat as I fell through the floor onto a soft and squirming surface. I was winded as I landed on the gun, my face killing me after getting a face full of mountain. I rolled over and propped myself against a peat wall of sorts. The soft squirming floor then started shouting Spanish at me and as I scrambled for my weapon it became more animated.

A drifting flare above lit up what appeared to be a face, I fired, this face shattered like an egg, showering the bunker and me in brain, skull, teeth and blood. The gunfire rendered me deaf as my ears rang. Out of the darkness another face and a pair of hands appeared and lunged at me, grabbing my throat and face. I grabbed at the wrists and attempted to prize them away.

"Jamie, Jamie" I screamed, muffled because my ears were still ringing.

This guys was screaming also, didn't have a clue what he wanted, probably help the same as me.

"Jamie, Jamie, help me"

I managed to get my right boot into his stomach area and push, whilst using my gloved hands to squeeze his wrists as hard as I could which loosened his grasp, and I managed to overpower him and pin him to the floor. Still in control of his hands, I head butted him, again, and again.

"You fuck, you fucker, fuck you" I spat in his face.

He was still screaming out for help.

I smashed my head into his face again, and again, and again.

"You bastard, fuck you, you fucking fuck" I roared.

I continued to plough my head into his bare face until he was silent.

I let go of his wrists, and his arms flopped to the floor. I scrambled back against the wall. Soaked with sweat, I caught my breath, and in the drifting light of the flares searched for my weapon.

1

San Carlos. To the casual observer, San Carlos sounds like a lovely warm holiday resort in the med or if you fancy being more exotic with your imagination, South America. Nothing could be further from the truth. The San Carlos in my life right now is bloody freezing, piss wet through, and just a shovels depth beneath my feet, more like the Somme. Our D-Day style landings was a far cry from what Hollywood had put onto screen, and thank Christ it was not on par with Omaha beach either. We'd been sat on HMS Intrepid for days and by this stage we had all had enough of being pitched and rolled all over the shop. When I joined the Parachute Regiment two years ago, it was all about being that warrior launching out the door of a Hercules, and a swift and aggressive strike on an overwhelmed enemy. This was more of a Royal Marine gig, all this assault ship and landing craft caper. We were meant to get ashore in the middle of the night, but due to us not being accustomed to this type of entry into battle, and one of the boys breaking a leg going arse over tit into the landing craft with all of his kit on, we found ourselves crammed in like sardines on this black and white crate of a thing they call a landing craft in broad daylight, not good! Just stood up in the craft, I was sweating my tits off, the amount of shit we were given to carry in this assault was a joke! On my person I had my helmet on, which to be fair was a lightweight design, intended for Paras, and not them horrible looking frying pan things the rest of the Army had to wear. We tended to fashion our helmet covers on our more revered airborne predecessors, the Fallshirmjeager, German Paratroopers.

We admired their no-nonsense approach to soldiering, just a shame from a Para view, they were not employed in a way they were most effective. I had scrim pulled tight over the top and a generous amount of black and nasty tape around the base to hold it in place, as for the rest of the Battalion; there were slight variations on the theme. Then there was my smock, a large, lightweight camouflaged jacked with built in hood and large pockets. This in itself weighed a ton with all sorts crammed in the pockets, clasp knife, chocolate, biscuits, notebook, pen, grenades, beret which we took everywhere, head over, which was a very crude olive green woollen sleeve of sorts that went over your head, hence the name, and acted as a scarf or balaclava. My lightweight windproof trousers, which were made of the same material as the smock, and included large pockets on the thigh area, which I had made sure were empty, so should I have to start charging machine gun nest from the get go, I could at least run, to a fashion. The boots, well let's just say this is an item of clothing that the British Army had not really addressed in any real depth. They were crap! Ankle high, cheap leather, useless at keeping the water out, but fantastic at keeping it in. To make it even worse, we had puttees, proper Dads Army kit, which we wrapped around the top of the boot, and after a short time in the field; they became just two sodden rags wrapped around your ankles.

My webbing, which was a canvas construction that had a belt, a yoke, which came over the shoulders of the wearer, and a series of pouches which had to accommodate all that you needed to fight the bad guys. Ammo, grenades, bayonet, water, food, shovel, some guys carried pick axes, and anything else that was of use in the assault. The lads varied their webbing slightly, depending on their role in the Battalion. My webbing was literally a carbon copy of the other lads in my section, yoke, belt, two ammo pouches, and five water bottle pouches in between, and on top was a canvas roll that held my wet kit and warm kit. The wet kit consisted of once again poor quality, a jacket and trouser combo that claimed to keep the water out, but that was fine if you were static, but if you had to move about abit, you sounded like a giant crisp packet, and you would sweat like a five dollar whore. As for the warm kit, it was a jacket and trouser combo that was quilted, and up until now in my army career, it did the job, it didn't keep me toasty, but kept the cold edge off me. The final piece to my South Atlantic Summer collection was my weapon, the General Purpose Machine Gun, know to all that have been involved with it, the Gimpy. This was a beast in itself, and just to remind me of the insatiable appetite this weapon had, 800 rounds of belt ammunition that had to accompany it.

To keep it easy to manage, I had 100 rounds in the gun and this was then wrapped around the body of it, and as for the remainder, that was wrapped around my shoulders and torso, giving me the Mexican bandit look, less the moustache, since bum fluff didn't qualify as facial hair, the more seasoned guys around me were displaying a serious amount of gringo tashes, which made them look even more sinister when plastered in camouflage cream. The powers that be felt it would be unwise to carry

Bergen's ashore, which was good to hear, since that would of been more of a drama, we had enough kit to carry as it was. A Bergen is a large rucksack construction that you carry the remainder of your gear, sleeping bags, spare clothing, extra food, and anything else you wish to bring with you. The plan was to recover our Bergen's from the beach once we had secured it and we could then settle down in our positions for the night. How they were going to get to the beach was anyone's guess, but I was just happy not to have to lug it ashore myself.

We came ashore without incident, and to be fair, it was a mixture of both relief and disappointment. There was abit of milling about on the shore, and then our section commander, John shouted out

"2 Section, grab your shit, let's go!"

John took the lead and led us off the beach and towards the high ground to the north of San Carlos, which was nothing more than a cluster of farm houses and fenced fields. Getting up here was a lick out, we literally just slogged it out up the hillside with speed being the priority, not so much, tactical awareness. Once we got onto the high ground looking north, there was then the usual everyone trying to be in charge, siting our trenches, and being moved around, again, and again. Finally, we stayed firm for longer than ten minutes and were then given the order to dig in. Our position was sited on a reverse slope, which to some would seem abit pointless, and I must admit, this was my first thought, but the method to the madness is, that should the enemy see you at a distance, they can stand off and hammer you with their long range weapons, but if they crest the hill, then see you, they are already in range of your weapons, hence the idea. The chance to get active was welcome, since the air was starting to chill me since my outrageous sweat fest on the landing craft, and then the Japanese death march up the hill. I was paired up with Jamie, who was my number two on the gimpy. He would essentially be an ammo donkey for me, since he would be lugging another 800 rounds for my weapon, plus his own allocation of ammo for his SLR, Self Loading Rifle, which was a long, magazine fed semi-automatic rifle, of 7.62mm calibre. This rifle was a man stopper on any given day, but due to its overall length could be a real pain in the arse when doing FIBUA on exercise, Fighting in Built up Areas.

Our section consisted of 8-men, including me, which comprised of a Section Commander, who was a Corporal. John was our commander, hard as woodpecker's lips, a no-nonsense operator who was part of the gringo tash gang. Covered in Para tattoos, he was the kind of guy you wouldn't want to meet in a dark alley. Despite this menacing profile, he was the ultimate family man, proud to be married, with three young children; he was very old school when it came to family values. He worked, his wife kept his house and children immaculate, and that was that, and to be fair, after attending a barbeque or two in his garden, it was clear to see his family was his number one priority in his life, but at work, John was all about the regiment, business is business, as he would put it. He was firm but fair with the guys in his section, he was the gaffer, and he wouldn't let any other Corporals outside the section mess us about. There was a time and a place when you would get a bollocking if you fucked up, but if it was uncalled for, he would defend you, whatever the rank of the person trying to have a pop.

Our section second in command, who was a Lance Corporal in rank, was Davo, totally different type of guy to John, laid back, casual, but an awesome soldier all the same. Davo would not entertain good cop, bad cop, when it came to running 2 section, John was the boss and Davo backed him in his decisions, that's how it worked in front of us, but off the radar, Davo would have a word with John now and again, should he have any reservations, and sometimes, John would u-turn on his decisions, this was rare however. Davo had no kids, but had a long term girlfriend, Sam, and to be fair, she was proper tasty, blonde, big tits, great body, and just lovely to chat to. She could handle herself, don't get me wrong, one night down the pub in Tidworth, Davo got jumped from behind whilst having a piss, and before we knew it had happened, Sam had battered his attackers, stiletto in each hand, you wouldn't want to be on the receiving end of her fury. I'm sure he will make an honest woman of her one day.

Jamie is as mad a box of frogs. He's one of them kids that has been left alone with the Coca-Cola too many times as a child. Face full of wholesome mischief, a smile that will melt the heart of any girl that meets him, but don't let that give you the impression he's a soft touch, our Jamie can handle himself, make no mistake. We joined together, and he is one of them bastards that makes everything to do with soldiering look easy. Our instructors in Aldershot had a devils own job trying to wear him out, for he was as fit as a butchers dog. He was due to go on his Fitness Instructor course before Maggie sounded the bugle to come down here and sort the Argies out, but he will just get it cracked when we get back. Born in Germany, since his dad was a soldier serving there at the time, but grew up in Portsmouth, in the Leigh Park area of the city, which is as rough as any estate you care to find back home, always scrapping at school, but had the smile that would get him into and out of all sorts of trouble. Just before joining the Army, there would be a series of visits to his home by angry fathers of pregnant daughters as they wanted to string the little bastard up, but Jamie's dad, always the mediator, would keep the wolf from Jamie's bedroom door. One evening, when Jamie was getting all tarted up to go out on the town, his dad pulled him up and sat him at the kitchen table, and read him the riot act, vowing that unless he got a grip of his shit, he would let the next angry father across the threshold and give him what he clearly needed. Jamie's cheeky smile and charm was not going to work on his dad, and Jamie did not have the bottle to call his dads bluff. The next day he went down the Army Careers office, and signed up for the Parachute Regiment. Not quite what his dad had in mind with sorting his life out, but proud nonetheless. The 7th March 1980 I met that crazy fool, day one week one at Depot Para, Browning Barracks, Aldershot, and you couldn't ask for a better mate, just don't leave your sister or mother in the same room as him for too long.

The other guys in the section, Kyle, Zane, Brandon, and Leighton were the more senior guys and had alot of time under their belts, having seen service in both Northern Ireland and Cyprus; they were also subscribers to the gringo club.

Kyle was from the South coast, but was taken to Malta as a baby. Malta is not the biggest country in the world, in fact it's smaller than the Isle of Wight, as for entertainment for a bored teenager, you had either sunbathing, or drinking and fighting the surprisingly large Russian population. During the holiday season, Kyle volunteered as a lifeguard and also had some form of medic training to keep him busy, but in the off season, the island was a ghost town, and that is where he would end up drinking with friends and it would usually end up in a brawl with drunken teenage Russians around a pool table or fruit machines. Kyle's folks sent him back to the UK to his Grandparents for a while to sort himself out, since it was clear that he would probably end up getting stabbed fighting the Russian kids, since it was not uncommon for them to be tooled up. It was during his time back in the UK, he decided the Army would offer him a life that would hopefully bring with it some satisfaction, so in 1976 he joined up, saw even more drunken brawling in his unit, since at the time the Battalion was serving in West Germany as part of a quick reaction force, driving about in Armoured Personnel Carriers, not quite what the

Paratrooper recruiting poster portrayed, but that's what their role was whilst out there. Waiting for the vast Russian hordes to come screaming across the North German plain got very boring very quickly, and in hindsight, if the Russians ever fancied a shot at the title they should of gone for it on pay day, since by the time they came in sight of British troops, the British would of been too pissed to even give a toss.

Zane's upbringing is not the most glamorous of childhood adventures. Youngest of two, his dad had an accident at work, so therefore was written off and kept the home fires burning and brought up the kids. Meanwhile his mum had to step up and assume the role of bread winner and it was not uncommon for her to hold down two, maybe three jobs at once just to keep bills paid, and Zane and his sister fed and clothed. Zane's school life was nothing much to shout about either, constantly in trouble, fighting on the way home, sometimes the odds were not in his favour and it wouldn't be the first time his sister would have to help him out in a tight spot, when a gang would circle him like hyenas. This in turn would cause his academic school life to suffer, arguing with teachers, bunking off, giving his parents a load of stick, always getting kicked out of the house, and ending up at his grandparents house which was luckily just a few streets away.

School was a lost cause on Zane, and one particular day when he felt a trip downtown was far more appealing than school, he walked past the Army Careers office. He rang the bell, and a rather overweight member of the Household Division answered. Stating his interest in joining, the recruiter let him in and made him a cup of tea. The earliest he could join was sixteen, and that was a few months off, and in any case, he would still need his parents' permission. The recruiter then pressed for which regiment he would like to join, Zane then had a walk around the large office at all the different regiments on offer in the form of posters. He liked the idea of being on Tanks, but that meant a life sentence in Germany, not what he was after. He also looked at the Guards, but standing like a lemon, as he put it, outside some posh gaff was not for him either. He was about to sit back down, when he caught in his sight line a poster for the Parachute Regiment, now this was more like it, jumping out of planes in the dead of night into the enemies backyard, with extra jump pay too, yes sir, Zane fell in love with this idea straight away. The recruiter appeared rather relieved this scruffy toe rag didn't ask for the Household Cavalry, and went to the filing cabinet to fetch all the relevant paperwork for entry into the

Parachute Regiment. Once at home, he poured the pile of paperwork onto the kitchen table announcing he was joining the Army. His parents were silent at first, then the silence was broken, his father stating that since he had trouble with doing as he was told at school, what made him think that the Army was going to put up with his shit either, more than likely the Army would knock it out of him. Zane shrugged his shoulders and asked for permission to join once he was sixteen, to which his parents merely looked at each other and shrugged, what's the worst that could happen? On his sixteenth birthday, 1974, his dad took him back to the careers office and signed the paperwork.

*

Brandon was somewhat of an unknown quantity, he pretty much kept himself to himself. He was a big fan of going home at the weekends, didn't drink much, which for a Para was a very rare breed indeed. He didn't have any tattoos that I knew of, bearing in mind the rest of us were pretty much walking adverts for the Regiment, his view was he was no less of a Paratrooper, tattoos or not, fair point! When it came to birds, he didn't act like a dog on heat when he got straight back off exercise like the rest of us, he just did his own thing, and maybe he had a bird back home, if he did, he didn't shout about it, and from what I can gather, he didn't have any kids. Just a very private guy. One night in the pub in Tidworth, one of the Mortar lads, came stumbling over, and accused Brandon point blank of being queer, don't get me wrong, I'm sure this guy was not the first to think it, but to blatantly poke the chest of the guy as you accuse him, you'd better have your facts straight. I almost choked on my beer when this happened as we were all together, just getting a few beers in mid-week, and before I could wipe my chin of beer, Brandon's head connected with this guys nose, and this guys face collapsed with the force of the head butt, this guys blood was all over the shop, spraying all over Brandon's face. Our broken friend was now on his knees, using both hands to keep hold of his blood and also muffling his own screams, but it wasn't muffled enough, as the barmaid let out a scream as the remainder of the Mortar lads came crashing through the bar towards us. No real time to prepare yourself for the ruck that was clearly imminent; I just took a deep breath and just got ready to deal with my first customer. It was at this time, John walked out of the bog, fag between his lips, doing up his flies, and the Mortar lads offensive screeched to a halt. Both groups eyed each other, and then looked at John, whose eyes narrowed to a glare, and he demanded what the problem was. One of the Mortar lads informed him that Brandon had smashed their boy in the face, John then looked at Brandon, who very calmly said this lad poked him in the chest and called him a queer. John rolled his eyes, put his fag out in the nearest ashtray, and told the Mortar boys, to pick up their boy, and fuck off back to their side of the bar, and to behave, which they did without hesitation. John was one of the old guard, no one messed with them boys, he held a kudos all of his own, he didn't need a gang to beat his drum for him, he could do it himself. As for Brandon, nice guy, just don't call him a queer.

Leighton was another Army brat born in Germany, his dad had served with the Royal Hampshire Regiment whilst out there, but one time on a tour in Ireland, his armoured Land Rover got hit with a Rocket Propelled Grenade, and this fucked up his dads hearing, who was then discharged on medical grounds. Now resettled in Havant, Leighton just had your run of the mill upbringing; his folks used his dad's compensation to set up their own sandwich delivery firm, and also a cafe. Leighton was all set to inherit the empire his folks had built, but from a very early age had his heart set on joining the Army. He was Army barmy, and bearing in mind he was being brought up on the outskirts of a city closely connected with the Navy, he was dead set on joining the Army. His folks had no real reservations, but his dad wanted him to join a unit that offered a trade and life skills, since he didn't want his boy to go down the same road as him, and have to scratch himself a living once he left the forces. Leighton's granddad had been in the Royal Engineers, and was a boiler maker, and upon leaving the Army, managed to land himself a Boiler making job in Portsmouth dockyard. Leighton wanted to travel and see action, and he was not going to find it boiler making. Leighton and his dad went down the Army Careers office, and Leighton asked for The Parachute Regiment. The recruiter asked why, Leighton said he saw news footage of them taking no shit in Northern Ireland and wanted some of that, the recruiter raised an eyebrow at his dad, who just shrugged his shoulders, and the paperwork started from there.

So this is us, not much to write home about, but with us all sat together, heavily armed and with enough attitude to start a small war of our own, we resembled something out of a Sven Hassel novel. It was early afternoon of our first day at war, and so far, we got soaked getting from ship to shore, and then that long slog up this bastard hill to our positions, and all we had to look forward to was an afternoon of landscape gardening, Army style.

Digging in was our priority now, since an Argentine counter attack was predicted within our first 24 hours ashore. In the back of my mind, getting killed or wounded was not a concern, but how long we were going to away for, a month?, a year? The World Cup was on soon and this pissed a lot of the boys off, as I'm sure there were a few Argentine soldiers moaning about why their masters wanted to invade during the World Cup as well.

2

Jamie with his pick; and me armed with a shovel, we started to carve ourselves a home in the hillside overlooking San Carlos water. We d removed the turf, and already we were sweating like lunatics, so we started to shed our gear, because we need to be down and ready as soon as possible, should we need to defend the beachhead that was already growing by the minute. Stripped down to just shirt and trousers, I paused to admire the view. All over the hillsides surrounding the bay wear hundreds of holes with troops milling about trying to get themselves sorted, it was only later on did I find out that the unit digging in off to the right of us across the bay was the Royal Marines, they'd had a bitch of a climb to their positions too, so our suffering was shared. On the water, it looked like a bloody marina, ships all over the place, to the point that it looked rather crowded. Helicopters with heavy under slung loads buzzing from ships to shore, getting the beachhead established. Pallets of kit, ammo, rations, fuel, you name it were already stacked up on the beach, very impressive.

"Fuck me, they're low"

As I looked to Jamie he was pointing up the valley, as I turned WHOOOSH BOOM! I dropped to my knees, ears ringing, and all I saw over the water were two shimmering orange glows going towards the ships in the bay, as they passed over the ships, huge geysers of water shot up straddling the ships directly underneath the orange glows. As my hearing returned, I could hear the cackle of automatic fire across the entire area. There was no one milling about their earthworks anymore, shit was going down, the enemy are here.

"Get in your fucking hole"

I looked over to where the abuse came from only to see John stood knee deep in his own hole pointing at me, and point sharply to the floor. I dropped like a stone, not through fear of getting a direct hit on my trench, but if John had to come over and repeat himself, the only direct hit would be on my chin. Jamie had dragged the gimpy in with him and we scrambled to get smocks and helmets on. We then got ready to take on the next jets that came over. The theory is that you are to put a huge amount of rounds into the air in the predicted path of the enemy aircraft, but that is the theory anyway. Fighter pilots are trained to fight other fighter pilots, and two chimps with a deckchair between them in a muddy hole is the least of their concerns. John appeared on the edge of our rather shallow trench, which scared the shit out of us,

"Right listen up, a few things are going wrong here, firstly, you are facing the wrong way, the ships are behind our position, and secondly, don't move anywhere as to attract the attention of these cunts"

He pointed up indication the enemy jets,

"Also, don't waste ammo trying to get em, got it?"

We nodded,

"Sit tight and I will keep you updated"

With that he then ran to Davo and Leighton's trench off to our right. Facing the brow of the hill made sense, but the real show was in the bay, me and Jamie took turns watching the show. The Navy was fighting for its life out on the water, throwing everything they had at the enemy jets. Huge geysers of water surrounded the ships, and the SS CANBERRA was sat slap bang in the middle, like a huge white turd on a snooker table, I didn't envy them one bit. These Argentine pilots were something else, they threw their machines around so low and fast, you couldn't help but admire their skill and bravery in equal measure, these guys were the racing drivers of the sky, Aryton Senna in a fighter jet springs to mind, crazy, brave, and dangerous. They seemed to go for the warships, not the CANBERRA, if only they knew troops were still aboard, it would be very grim for us. The Navy were starting to clock up the kills now they had recovered from the initial shock of the attacks, one jet in particular came in real low and it appeared to just disintegrate in a hail of machine gun fire and what was left of the airframe hit the water and cart wheeled below the surface, scratch one racing driver, but these bastards kept coming, pummelling the ships, who with little room to manoeuvre, just had to sit there and scrap it out. John came over to our trench again, this time at a more casual pace,

"Keep digging, they are after the ships, in case you haven't noticed".

So with that, we cracked on digging, totally unmolested, whilst the Navy was literally trying to stay afloat. We got our trench deeper, and so far, no issue with water coming in, since the water table was so near the surface, even on the high ground. We had no overhead protection, just the turfs wed removed at the start, but without timber to hold it up, it was no good at this stage. The light was starting to fade, and the Argentine air force had had enough for the day, as I'm sure the Royal Navy was glad to hear, but they'll be back, no doubt about it. Looking at the ships, some of them had columns of smoke coming from torn holes in the sides of them and allsorts. One was clearly on fire, and this would continue into the night, I only hoped that all those onboard were ok, and casualties were light. At last light, John came back over to us and said to take just weapons and mags in pockets to the rear of the company position, since our Bergens had arrived. I grabbed the gimpy and some extra link just in case, Jamie with SLR and mags in his pockets, we made our way to the rear of the position where we came across a line of tractors and large trailers. The residents of San Carlos settlement, who by the looks of things, lived like farmers, had offered their services to the Battalion, by lugging all our heavy stores to where we needed them, fantastic. Great idea, don't get me wrong, but when you are trying to find your Bergen in the dark, amongst a pile of a hundred odd Bergen's, tests the sense of humour of the most hardy soldiers. We had guys cursing, some throwing gear about, some even giving up altogether, and leaving it till first light. After a long search, I entertained the idea, and put it to Jamie,

"fuck that, put it this way Archie, keep warm looking for it now, and when you've found it, you know you're going to stay warm",

He had a point, keep searching. It paid off; we found our bergens and made our way back to our position. Sleeping in the field, especially in a war like scenario is not camping by any stretch of the imagination. You have to sleep fully clothed, just in case the bad guys pay you a visit in the night, and you can jump out of your sleeping bag and start shooting. You can however concede a few items of clothing, I would take my boots off and put my trainers on when in my bag, but I would keep my boots with me inside with me so they didn't go stiff or freeze if they were left outside, so if I had to get out in a hurry, I had footwear on to deal with any problems, and besides, it was a small victory to get time out of them horrible boots. Then there was your quilted suit, you would get cold very quickly if you got out of your bag after spending the night with it on, so what you did was take it off, and keep it in there with you, which made life rather cosy, and when you had to get up, you put it back on as normal, and felt the benefits straight away, these little charms of info made life as comfortable as possible in these conditions, as there would be times in your career when you just had to grin and bear the weather in whatever you was wearing.

We got settled, but no sleep was to be had, the crazy events of the day we just had was still racing through our minds.

"You know what?" Jamie posed

"If their Army is anything like their Air force" he looked at me and winked "we are gonna miss the World Cup".

He had a point, we'd have a scrap on our hands if their soldiers were as crazy and brave as their pilots. It was not our turn on watch yet so we arranged ourselves so we were facing the ships in the bay. The wind picked up, and was now howling over the hillside, and I could just make out the sound of helicopters working like mad to get as much of our recourses ashore by first light. We laid there, looking over the water, paying particular attention to the ship that was still ablaze in the bay, and at the same time we just chatted about nothing in particular, when there was a huge explosion on the burning ship, it was a few seconds later when the huge boom reached us, and the ship didn't seem to burn anymore. Jamie looked at me and winked, then pulled the hood of his sleeping bag over his head, stating that I was boring him now, and was to shut up. With friends like him, I didn't need enemies.

"Rise and shine you pair of homos."

I pulled open a rather frozen stiff sleeping bag hood, to be greeted with the menacing grin of John, whose heavily cam creamed face and outrageous gringo tash made it all the more of a wakeup call.

"Danny and the Boss are doing the rounds this morning, shit went down out to our front last night with Patrols and C Company, so he's going to brief us up on the facts, get out of your pits and get your admin squared, understand?"

We both nodded, and he stood up and went on his way. We slowly emerged from our sleeping bags like a butterflies trying to shed its cocoon, it was fucking freezing. The early morning light was just starting to emerge over the horizon, the wind was howling like a banshee, and a frost had set in because it had been a clear night, I'd rather have cold then wet and cold any day. We got to our feet and straight away the cold hit us, so I dug into my sleeping bag, and felt for my quilted suit. Slipping it on was like a gift from the gods, and all around the company position we could see guys doing the same, stamping their feet, even doing abit of drill, just to get warmed up. Admin, as John put it, is administration of your weapons, your kit, then you, in that order. There has to be a compromise on this though, because of the entire company strips and cleans their weapons at the same time, and the bad guys rock up in front of us, things will not go well for us. The way we get around this is by working with your trench buddy, I strip and clean the gimpy, while my beautiful assistant puts the kettle on and acts as chef. I unloaded the gimpy, and then went about stripping it down into its basic working parts, removing and build up of ice and frost, and inspecting for any signs of rust. I remove my gun gleaning kit out of my Bergen, which holds all what I need to keep this beast up and running. Once happy all is in order, I apply a light coating of gun oil to all metal bearing surfaces, and then rebuild the gun. Just to make sure the thing will work when we need it most, I carry out a function test, to ensure the safety mechanism and firing mechanism work when deliberately applied. To round this function off, I inspect the 100 round belt I've had attached to it for the last 24 hours is free of rust and isn't kinked and replace it back it the weapon, job done. With this chore complete, I now assume the duties of chef so Jamie can do the same with his SLR.

The rations we are issued are designed to feed the fighting man in constant action, so 24 hours worth of food and supplements comes to about 7000 calories. To the casual observer this appears rather extreme, but average Joe in the street doesn't have to carry between 70-120lbs of weapons and equipment everywhere with him, and on top of that, have to fight with it on as well. The rations we have at this stage are designed for troops operating in and Arctic environment, where snow is in abundance. This is not the case here right now, no snow, loads of frost, but not enough to supplement the British military machine at San Carlos right now. We have to supplement the rations in order to cook from the water bottles in our webbing, and here lies the problem, so to deal with this, we have been issued with sterilizing tablets so we can use the local stream water around us. It makes the water safe, don't get me wrong, but the water is almost black, and it tastes like you are drinking swimming pool water once the tablets have dissolved. Vile.

Breakfast in the ration packs is a very basic fare, porridge of some description, and a mixture of sausage, bacon and beans. In a roadside cafe, this sounds quiet appealing, but when you get it Army style, it has all the appeal of dog food. To wash this lovely feast down, we have hot chocolate mix, or tea and coffee. Lunch consists of a mixed selection of energy tablets, biscuits that a dog wouldn't even eat, and bars of chocolate that a child would ignore. And to wrap up, we have dinner, which is not too bad, to be fair, normally a type of stew mix, or even pasta based. The rations do what they say on the tin, no thrills, bulk fuel. A real test of endurance for the soldier is having the same menu, day in, day out, for weeks. The next phase of our admin period was shaving and inspecting your feet, since being clean shaving has not won a war on its own, but soldiers with bad feet could well change the outcome of any campaign. You've only got to read articles from the First World War to appreciate the need for decent footwear for fighting men, but this was still an ongoing issue, cheap massed produce boots that clearly don't have to be worn by the bean counters in Whitehall. Shaving for me and Jamie was a brief, weekly flirtation with a razor, since we didn't really grow any, but the gringo gang had a real time of it in this cold harsh weather, when only a wet shave would do the job. My feet were in good shape since Id slept with my trainers on, so a quick change of socks, and back into the boots with minimum fuss. Admin sorted, breakfast cleared away, Bergen's repacked, we then settled down to another day defending Queen and Country. The sun was higher in the sky now, but no less cold, Jamie nudged my arm and pointed out into the bay. The ship that exploded in the night was still afloat, but in a bad way. She was very low in the water, the middle of it was as good as missing, the coal black smoke of yesterday had now been replaced by a light grey column drifting into the sky as if to mark her last stand, very sad, I felt for the Navy, stuck out in the bay, at least on land, on your own two feet, you had a say in the matter, more or less. She couldn't stay afloat much longer surely, no more boats went to her aid, and she just sat there, waiting to die.

John was on his way over, with two other guys, as they got closer we saw it was Tony, the Platoon Commander, or Boss as we called him more informally, and Danny, our Platoon Sergeant. Danny was another one of the old guard, tough, no nonsense, and lifetime friend of John; I think they went through training together. As for the boss, he had a couple of years under his belt, in fact, I think he came to the Battalion the same time as me, but he had to go through Sandhurst, since he joined the Army as an Officer, and if I'm honest, he was only about a year or so older than me and Jamie as well. As they got near our trench, we stood up to greet them, straight away; Danny waved us to sit down,

"Relax boys, just doing the rounds",

And this put us at ease straight away. Back in Tidworth, you could either expect reward or a bollocking from Danny, especially if wed pissed him off during the course of the week, fighting down town, not shaving before work, smashing up our accommodation during a drink filled weekend, basically anything that would have him receiving a bollocking from Dale, the Company Sergeant Major, who was the right hand man of Justin, our Company Commander. Straight away we could see there was a different issue to address here.

"Guys" Tony began, "just to keep you in the picture, Patrols were out to the North of us last night, recceing a possible site for a drop zone for both stores and troops, should our stay here be long term"

Patrols were shortened for Patrols Company, who was the reconnaissance company for our Battalion, our early warning eyes and ears essentially.

"During the night" he continued, "they ambushed a platoon from C Company who just so happened to be patrolling the same real estate, unknown to Patrols"

Me and Jamie just looked down at the ground shaking our heads, John piped up "how did this happen?"

"C Company's patrol programme was not scrutinised before they went out", he continued" if it was, they could of avoided Patrols who were the primary call sign out in front of our positions, a couple of C Company lads have been bashed up pretty bad, they will live, but their war is over, maybe even their careers".

We couldn't believe it, we've only just got here, and we are shooting each other up, and no sign of enemy ground forces yet.

"Hey" Danny snapped us back to reality, "it happens, won't be the last time, besides, lets deal with the task at hand, are you guys ok?, feet okay?",

We nodded, "good, right, we've gotta shoot, we can't be out in the open for too long, know what I mean"

Pointing up as he finished his sentence, as they moved off towards Davo and Leighton's trench, Danny called back

"How are you guys fixed for ammo? Did you get much off yesterday?"

Before we could answer, John waved his hand dismissively "told em not to bother, the fuckers are too fast", Danny nodded, and they then continued on, we started digging through our webbing for our brew kit.

Sometime later, Jamie piped up

"Hey check that out"

I looked up to Jamie pointing into the bay, the broken ship from last night had finally given up the fight, her back broken, all that was pointing above the water line was her bow and stern, she had lost her fight for life.

Off to our right, we heard the crackling of machine gun fire, and John, The Boss and Danny jogging past our trenches on their way back to theirs,

"Round two", Danny shouted, as two jets screamed across the length of our Battalion frontage then banked left into the bay, in order to give the Navy another pasting. We sat tight with our brews, with the best ringside seats in the house, for what we thought would be a repeat of yesterday. How wrong we were, the Navy gunners had their shit squared for this round, and we're not going to get caught napping on this one, they were waiting for Aryton and his mates. The Argentine pilots were no less crazy or brave than yesterday, but their efforts didn't come to much this time round since we now had Surface to Air missiles all set up on shore and the gunnery of the sailors manning the rail on board got very deadly overnight. Aryton and Co were dropping like flies, and those that survived their runs were disappearing out of site with smoke trailing from their machines. Where were these Harriers we were meant to have? Little did I know that the pilots that came into the bay to attack our ships were in fact the survivors of some tasty dogfights with our Harriers who intercepted them on their run in from the Argentine mainland. I guess there were more of them than there was of us, so some were bound to slip through the net. By early afternoon, the attacks had all but faded away as they had taken major losses during the morning, we couldn't get too cocky and start larking about outside our trenches, but the pressure was off, at least for the time being. Our next trench visitor was Davo, all full of smiles as usual, as he rocked up, he started to chuckle,

"Good to see your abortion of a trench looks as bad as mine",

He had a point; our trench looked more like a ragged shell hole, rather than a trench to NATO specifications.

"Listen, pallets and timber and shit is getting brought up from the farm, you're gonna get a pallet and some timber to sort out your OHP (Over Head Protection), go down to Dales position and he will give you your timber and pallet."

Happy with that, nothing beats having a roof over your head, even if it's just a pallet with turf on it. Weapons and mags only, we trotted down to Dale's trench, which he shared with his Signaller, Robin, who had the wonderful task of moving about with his Bergen, all the time, since he had to man pack the radio set everywhere Dale went, treat yourself. We were part of 5 Platoon, and we were dug in forward right on the Company position, with 4 Platoon forward left, so our Company had a two platoon frontage in which to fight enemy ground forces, should they make an appearance. Just behind where both Platoons linked up in the middle, was our Company Commander, Justin's trench, whom he shared with his Signaller and pack mule, Trevor. About one 100 metres behind Justin was 6 Platoon, who would act as a reserve, and they would basically bolster the main line, should us and 4 platoon have trouble holding the enemy at bay. They also acted as a counter attack force, so should the enemy not have their act together whilst trying to push through the main line, 6 platoon would deploy left or right of the Company line and beat the enemy back to take pressure off the two lead platoons. Just behind 6 platoon's position was Dale's trench, sited in such a position, so he could read the battle 4 and 5 were fighting and put 6 in such a position that was of use to Justin as he would direct the defence of our position. As we got to Dales trench, we could see once again some of the tractors from yesterday, along with their huge trailers, off loading pallets and timber to the small queue of customers forming at the rear.

"Alright lads?" Dale winked

"Yes sir" we replied, he pulled out a flask, from his trench and poured himself a brew,

"Wanna sip?" we accepted his offer and I tell you what, this tea was a gift from the gods, and this was not ration tea at all.

"Were did you get this" I asked, he just winked at me, tapping his nose with his gloved hand

" never you mind Archie boy, never you mind, besides, grab your pallet, and get yourself sorted, them tossers might come back with ground troops on the menu"

With that we moved to the back of the trailer and received our pallet and this haggard old guy that rambled away at us, then burst out laughing, which then turned into a hacking cough. We just smiled and took our pallet and two planks of timber and started lugging them back up to our trench. 6 Platoon were as good as finished with their trench upgrade, since them jammy bastards were the nearest when the tractor arrived.

"Was that English that old boy said or what?" Jamie asked out loud,

"Fuck knows" I shrugged," It sounded either Cornish or South African to me",

Jamie adjusted the planks to a more comfortable position,

"Whatever it was" he continued, "proper fucked up".

I just grunted as I was slowly getting the hump with the pallet already.

We wasted no time in getting our roof on, and very carefully placing on the turfs wed put to one side from yesterday. We got inside and had to make sure, we could fight this position if we had to with both the gimpy and SLR pointing out the firing slit, it was abit tight but, I suppose you have to just piss with the cock you've got. We even walked out to the front of our position and admired it from the front, not too bad. We ventured further away towards the crest of the hill and peered over the top before committing ourselves to skyline. As the hill dropped slowly away on the other side, there were miles and miles of nothing, total bare arsed open ground.

"They're out there somewhere, and if they're not gonna come to us, then I guess it will be us going to pick a fight with them"

I looked at Jamie, who was looking back at our position, Dale was stood at the back of our trenches, talking with The Boss, Danny, and John was waving at us to get back to him rapido. We jogged back down off the skyline towards the group that was growing rapidly, since the entire platoon was gathering around Dale,

"Shit is going down mate" Jamie mumbled as we approached the group. Everyone was taking a knee in front of Dale, less The Boss, Danny and the Section Commanders.

"Listen up guys, the OC (Officer Commanding, official title for Justin), is away at orders right now, since things have all now changed, and we need to act now."

He paused to allow that to sink in.

"Brigade had planned for us to take several bounds east towards the main defensive area around Port Stanley over the next couple of days, using Chinooks"

Chinooks are large, double rotored helicopters that can lift heavy stores, or almost a Company strength of troops in one lift.

"Earlier, a container ship called the Atlantic Conveyor, was sunk in an air raid, with all but one of the Chinooks on board"

Groans now spread through the group, Dale raised a hand to keep order,

"Brigade plan for us and the Commandos to move east, on foot later today. More details will follow, so get your selves squared for Tabbing, and I will get more info to you as I find out more, look sharp boys, this shit just got very real".

Back at our trench, we set about getting ready for what was on the cards as a bloody long tab. Tab in Army speak means Tactical Advance to

Battle, carrying literally what you need to fight the enemy, and no luxuries. John came up to our trench.

"No Bergens for this one, be prepared to be away from them for at least 48 Hours, once you've packed your shit get your Bergens stacked up behind 6 platoon, Danny will be marking the Platoons Bergens, so make sure you put yours in the right pile".

As he trotted off to see Davo next door, we set about getting ready. Firstly, weapons and ammo. It was all to be taken, gimpy, ammo, spare parts wallet, gun cleaning kit, spare barrel, two High Explosive grenades, two smoke grenades, one White Phosphorous Grenade. This gear on its own weighed enough, and then we had to make sure we had enough water and rations to sustain us, and we rammed as many of the set meals we had in our Bergens into our webbing, and the chocolate, biscuits and sweets went into our smock pockets. Then came clothing, I was already wearing a shirt, green Army woollen jersey, a quilted jacket and my smock, but I would be stripping down to just shirt and smock for the march since I would be soaked in sweat within a mile, so the quilted gear would be going back into the canvas roll along with my waterproofs, my jersey and poncho sheet would be going into the barrel bag us gunners got to lug as well. My poncho consisted of a large sheet of waterproof material, not too dissimilar to the waterproofs issued to us, but it had a drawstring hood in the middle so it too could be a waterproof jacket of sorts, but it also had ringed eyelets at the corners so with small tent pegs and elasticated hook bungees which you see in various colours when you go camping, you can erect a temporary shelter, it won't keep you warm, but it should keep the wind and rain off you. All that was then stuffed into the barrel bag also. Last to be found a home, was three pairs of socks, one set in my inside pocket, the remaining two sets into the barrel bag. Not happy that my trainers and sleeping bag were going to be left in the Bergen for now, I then shouldered my Bergen, and set off down to the rear of the Company position to drop it off. There was troops everywhere, sorting the Bergen piles out for each platoon, grabbing last minute bits and pieces from them, or stuffing gear into them, since the owner felt he didn't need it, or didn't want to carry it. I found our platoon pile and put mine down next to it.

"The locals are going to pull all our heavy gear for us in their trailers, bloody nice of em don't you think?" Danny commented,

I just nodded and smiled. Further down the hill, towards where Battalion Headquarters were located, I could see a lot of our heavy weapons and their ammo being loaded onto tractor trailers, since the Fire Support Company guys would be tabbing also, but without their monstrous loads, such as their Mortars, Milan Anti-Tank weapons, and the Heavy 30. Cal machine guns. As I was making my way back up to my position, John had already got the section into a huddle, so I got a jog on expecting a bollocking for being late. John looked round to me,

"Archie, park your arse there"

I knelt down next to Brandon who just winked at me, as he offered me a sip of his brew.

"Right guys, in a minute, we are going to start tabbing east towards, a place called Teal Inlet, about 40 Kilometres away"

Someone gave out a low whistle,

" Patrols will be leading, so they can give the Battalion advance warning of any trouble we may encounter on the route. The ground we will be covering will be hard going, so watch where you place your footing, don't want anyone busting an ankle, the OC intends for us to rest for 5 in every hour, the pace won't be outrageous, but with all our gear, and the terrain, it won't be a stroll either. Order of March, 6 Platoon will lead, followed by Company HQ, 5 Platoon, then finally 4 Platoon. Don't collapse your trenches, they will be occupied by follow on troops, fuck knows who, but leave them as they are. Once you've got your gear on just sit in front of your trenches so I can see that you are ready, any questions?"

There was none, I think we were all just get our minds ready for a bloody long night.

Me and Jamie got our kit on and took the time to ensure it was going to be as comfortable as possible for the night ahead. First of all, I made sure my green woollen jersey was taken off in preparation for the march, and for a brief period took a look at the Parachute wings sewn on the upper right arm. If you had completed the Basic Parachute Course at RAF Brize Norton, you earned the right to wear your wings on the upper right arm of all of your military clothing, with the exception of your fitness gear.

"Well Archie boy" I said to myself," this is one of them times where you need to be careful of what you wish for".

You busted a gut in training to wear these babies, and become a fully paid up member of the Parachute Regiment, and this is what you get, the kudos of being a paratrooper, but the harsh, tough missions that are part of the job description for a tough unit. Truth be known, this also went for the Commandos dug in across the bay, they had a somewhat longer history than us, but they all carried kudos of being a Commando, and what came with it. Both the Commandos and us had a long professional rivalry, but don't tell anyone I said this, they are a good, tough bunch of operators. Jersey now stowed in my barrel bag, I then refitted my smock ensuring all the pockets were done up, and the right kit was stowed for easy access, field dressing, morphine, which was issued prior to the landings, so should we have a casualty, you gave the casualties his morphine, and not your own. Notebook and pen, biscuits, chocolate and sweets, which I could shove in my gob on the move, head over, socks, beret, clasp knife, smoke grenade. Then on went my webbing, which was fully packed out with the rest of my fighting gear. On top of that went the 600 rounds of belt ammunition for the gimpy, so I was sporting the Mexican bandit look for this march, 100 on the gun, and the remaining 100 was crammed into the barrel bag, which was the next item to go on, and I could already feel the strain on ones legs without even taking a step yet. I then pulled the straps tighter and jumped up and down to make sure nothing was going to rattle or fall off, once happy I then slumped on the ground next to Jamie, who was already kitted up and was slowly putting fresh cam cream onto his face. I positioned myself next to him, with the gun and my helmet along side, and I then began to apply fresh cam cream also, once complete we just looked out into the bay, and the surrounding hillsides, watching other units, getting their shit sorted for the move east.

It was about mid afternoon now, and we would start to lose light shortly. Looking left and right of me, I could see the other lads in the Company, sat outside their trenches putting on fresh cam cream, smoking, picking their noses, scratching their balls, some just put their heads back onto their gear and got in a kip before the order to move out would come soon enough. John moved up and down the Section line, in just his smock carrying his rifle, informing us that Patrols had already set off from Battalion HQ and once they began to establish the route east, C Company will then follow, then us, then Fire Support with the tractors full of their gear, then A Company. The Bergens would follow at some point, when the CQMS could get forward to Teal Inlet. The CQMS is the Company Quartermaster Sergeant, who is a Colour Sergeant in rank. Phil was a nice guy, very can do, along with his staff, whose job it was to ensure B Company got bombs, bullets, food and water on a regular basis, he could also pull a few string and acquire some little luxuries, depending where we were, such as cans of pop or bags of crisps, even bread, these little things go along way for a soldier living on the bare basics to sustain him on operations, a good CQMS is abit of an Arthur Daley, wheeling and dealing, but never at the expense of the men he had to sustain in the field.

Speaking of logistics, down by the water's edge, I was completely blown away by the sheer volume of supplies that was piling up for us to fight this campaign; I'd never seen stores in this volume ever in my career so far. Pallets and pallets of ammunition, more than I care to count, grenades, mortars, missiles, rations, medicine, are but just a few of the items stockpiled down there, helicopters still working like angry bees getting the pollen from the ships to the shore as quick as possible, I'm no pilot by any stretch, but I'm sure the flying hours rule had been thrown out of the window long ago, they were just going for it nonstop. Why Ayrton and his gang never spotted this pile of gear is anyone's guess, just think, on well placed bomb or gun run could of ended our land campaign right there on the beach, crazy!

3

"Prepare to move!"

Danny yelled so that the entire Platoon could hear him. I welcomed this order to be honest, since having just a shirt on under my smock; the chilled air was starting to creep in. Jamie, being somewhat more agile than the fat Mexican next to him managed to get to his feet then helps me up. Once up we quickly adjusted our kit so it was a comfortable as could be, since I'm sure the manufacturers hadn't designed it with these loads in mind. I then with the aid of Jamie, I half knelt, half squatted like a geriatric and grabbed the carrying handle of the gimpy and hanging on it was my helmet. I fitted the gimpy so that the gun was across my mid-drift and the sling was over my head and across my shoulder blades, which initially wasn't too bad an arrangement, since it evened out the load distributed across my frame. The helmet went on, and this Para was ready to go find the bad guys. We started off downhill which I found rather bizarre, since we had to climb out of San Carlos initially, but at the end of the day, I just followed the guy in front as we shook out into our order of march, everyone was still a lot of stop, start. Ahead of us on the high ground opposite, the Commandos were making their way down hill as well, and making their way to our left towards where the valley came to a narrow apex. We starts to swing around to the left and hand rail the water course out of the bay, the ground underfoot was already showing the signs of surface water, and bog, as we waded almost ankle deep in it, and before I knew it, my feet were soaked, great!

The tab up out of San Carlos was already having me get a sweat on as my back and neck were starting to get wet with exertion. The Company had formed two columns as we made our way up out of the bay, the Commandos opposite us on the other side of the river had done the same, but then I noticed they had Bergens, the whole lot, I wasn't sure if that was a good or bad move, since we would cover ground quicker than them, but they had sleeping bags to climb into should they stop for a while, we would have to see. I also noticed that while we had helmets on, they wore their green berets, good move in my book, I was starting to really get a sweat on, and the bloody barrel bag was already getting on my tits. I adjusted the gimpy to take pressure off my back and then I noticed up front, both Paratrooper and Commando who were gimpy gunners had it over their shoulder, holding onto the butt group, the part of the weapon you put in the shoulder when firing, that was good enough for me, so I quickly joined the masses, and it did make movement easier since I could now swing my left arm in order to propel myself forward. Someone up front went arse over tit into the bog, and some of the lads let out a cheer, but the lad in question just swore like a man possessed as a couple of the guys pulled him to his feet, I did not want to fall over, entertaining as it may be to my mates. As we climbed higher, I was in full sweaty mess tab mode now, but I was warm through exercise, and not looking forward to the night ahead, not because of what we had to do, but it was looking like it was going to be a clear night, and that meant only one thing, cold.

The going started to level out as we got out of the valley, we continued to hand rail the river on our right and the Commandos were doing the same on the other side. Their pace was much slower than ours, probably due to their loads, but maybe their bosses didn't want to kill them before they encountered the enemy. Our lot however, had a rocket up their arses, and really set a lick of a pace, it wouldn't of surprised me if the guys leading were having a pissing competition with the Commandos up front, but I wasn't in the mood for any of that shit, I was more worried about turning an ankle, or falling face first in to bog that seeped out from the river left and right of it. All of a sudden the pace slowed to a crawl, and the word came down the line to take five. We were stood ankle deep in a water logged bog, so the most I could do at this stage was take the gun off my shoulder rest the butt group on a semi dry tuft of grass and lean with both hands on the end of the barrel. The Commandos did the same; we were close enough to them to exchange glances and gestures. The Marine opposite me who was leaning on his gimpy in the same fashion, looked at me and shook his head,

"Who's idea was this? "

I wasn't sure if he was on about the march, or his boss's decision to carry Bergens.

"Mate, proper lick out" I replied,

He grinned and adjusted a strap before he stood up straight. We then got the order to get ready to move, and already the Commandos started to shuffle forward again. We then stared to move again, pretty steady at first, but before long the pace got stupid again. We literally hand railed the river, which is easy on the navigation, don't get me wrong, but the river at certain points would almost double back on itself, and with all this kit on, was becoming a pain in the arse, that forty kilometres they stated, that is probably in a straight line, at this rate, we will probably clock up about sixty by the time we got to Teal Inlet. We got to a prominent right turn in the river course and I noticed that our Battalion then led off in a almost straight pair of lines out into open country, whilst the Commandos got wet crossing the river and headed off North, what the fuck! Whoever makes these plans clearly don't look at many maps I'm sure. I was to find out later, that these Commandos were heading to a settlement called Douglas, about fourteen kilometres from their river crossing. Their job was to deal with any enemy in that area, then move around to Teal, our objective. Apparently this was the plan all along, but with Chinooks, instead, the plan stayed the same, but it would be done in the ankle high, soaking wet, leather personnel carriers, our boots.

The Marine I exchanged words with a little while back had just had his freezing cold foot spa for the day as he passed in front of me,

"All the best mate "he said, "Last one to the bar in Stanley ",

I winked at him,

"Take care mate, I will save you my trench in Teal ".

The Battalion then head East, North East towards Teal. The ground started to get dryer and more firm underfoot, then the clowns up front started to hug the low ground, being all tactical and shit and where there is low ground there is water. About half an hour after we left our Commando friends at the river crossing, word come down the line to take thirty and get a brew and scoff on. Me and Jamie found a raised bank of sorts and slumped against it. I was pissed wet through with sweat, and to be honest, I couldn't be arsed to get all this gear off, but Jamie, being as agile as a cat, was out of his gear and had deployed his brew kit and scoff, and the water was on the go. I shouldn't have been such a lazy shit, but all I wanted was to sort my socks out, I had plenty of grub to stuff my face with in my smock. Jamie scrambled around behind me,

"Lean forward, I'll get you a scoff out",

I did as he asked, and he rifled through my webbing and found me some goulash and hard tack biscuits, I then leant back as he continued to play chef. The light was fading and the cold was starting to set into our chilled bodies, so before I went completely into crow mode, this being a condition of idleness, and you have all the demeanour of a new recruit, a crow. I lifted my right boot, undid the laces and slipped my boot of then pulled a rather wet sock off. I then inspected my foot, it was all pruned like I'd been in the bath too long, and I then ringed my sock out and placed it back on, then re-fitted my boot. This mere act of ringing out my sock made life feel a lot more comfortable, believe it or not. I then repeated the process with my left foot. Once my foot care was complete, dinner was served, I tore open the bag of goulash carefully not to spill any of the hot sauce on my smock, and taking my pack of biscuits, I crushed them up and then sprinkled them in to goulash, which basically doubled the size of the meal. From my inside pocket, stashed next to my spare socks was my spoon, which I robbed from the galley on the CANBERRA, with that, I tucked in, thanking Jamie for sorting out his fat, lazy, arsehole of a friend. He winked as he ploughed through his scoff, not too sure what he had, it wasn't around long enough to be inspected. Food done, when then just savoured our rest time share the Hot Chocolate he prepared also, Jamie would make someone a fine wife someday.

When word comes down the line to get on our feet, I was glad due to the fact it was really getting cold now, since there wasn't a cloud in the sky, and at this twilight stage of dark setting in, the sky was just crammed with stars, and you could see your own breath in the cold air. Once on our feet, we quickly adjusted ourselves, so for at least a while; our kit was as comfortable as possible. Our column started to shuffle off and I quickly adjusted the gimpy on my right shoulder. Looking at the guys in the column up ahead reminded me of the footage and photos of German troops in the vast expanse of Russia advancing towards the Volga. The cold that engulfed us just added to the atmosphere of this image I had in my head of the Eastern Front all them years ago. The pace started to really open up now, and earlier I thought it was the pace setters trying to prove a point to the Commandos. Sweat soon made a comeback under the weight of my kit and the pace of the march. The terrain didn't help much either, it reminded me of Sennybridge, where we conducted most of our exercises back home, open moorland, hardly ever flat, and rough tussocks of grass that if caught wrong could turn an ankle, and even trip you over. Water was present on the surface also, so it wasn't long before my feet were soaked once again. I wasn't sure if we were smashing the route out on a straight compass bearing to Teal or those leading our column just didn't care for the guys, who were really feeling it will all their kit on. We went up and down these short but harsh gradients instead of skirting around them, there was no middle ground as the pace was a lick, and on the high ground there was the harsh babies-heads, what the Army would call the tussock grass, and in the low ground, you had to slog your way through bog and surface water.

After what seemed like hours, we stopped for a breather. Soaked in sweat, I slumped to the floor and fished out a water bottle, despite the cold night, the water in my bottle was refreshing, since I was finding the tab hard work. I wasn't alone, guys who were known for their tabbing prowess were feeling the pace, big gaps started to appear in the line, where guys started to flag under their loads. A few guys had fallen out of the march some distance back, probably due to ankle injuries, or maybe even being exhausted, no one stuck around to even see if they were ok. I just hoped the Battalion medics were dealing with them, and the casualties were getting put into the trailers being pulled by the locals. It was now getting really cold, even more so as my sweat started to get cold and dry. I pulled out my black leather gloves and slipped them on, they gave me some instant relief, as it got my hands out of the increasingly biting wind that had picked up. I stuffed some chocolate into my mouth that I had fetched from my smock pocket, leant over and nudged Jamie, and offered him the rest of it.

"Cheers mucker," he nodded, "I'm chinned, and this is a lick out"

I just grinned at him.

"Hopefully there are no bad guys at Teal," I added," and we can get some kip instead"

He chuckled, despite the fact that the chances of enemy forces being at our destination could be a very real prospect. If anyone was going to encounter an enemy presence at Teal, it would be the Patrols Company lads. They were ahead of the main bulk of the Battalion on this march, both proving the route to Teal, but also hopefully giving us advance warning of any enemy they encounter on the route or at our destination. If enemy were spotted on the route. The patrols lads would initially keep a low profile and assess what strength they were, and what type of weapons they had and stuff like that. They wouldn't kick things off straight away, unless it was an opportunity too good to miss, for example, all the bad guys were in bed or something like that, they would report over the radio to the CO, the Commanding Officer of our Battalion, Charlie. Charlie would receive the information from Patrols and if he still had reservations he would make us sit tight, and go forward to see the bad guys for himself. He would then come up with a plan, and dish it out to the companies, who would do the fighting, Patrols would keep eyes on during the planning phase and drip feed information to the companies, so they had up to date information in real time. We ended up sitting on that windswept, freezing cold hillside for some time, and I was tempted to get this kit off and get my warm kit on, but me being the lucky guy I was, as soon as I got all comfy, we would be off again. I carried out a damage assessment of my aching cold wet frame. My shoulders ached from the gimpy, during the course of the night I was changing which shoulder would carry the gun, my hips started to get sore, since my sweat had soaked through my shirt and smock, and had now soaked into the canvas belt of my webbing. The canvas when wet, shrunk and also got very stiff, so after a while the rubbing would create sores, which made the march all the more unpleasant. I started to get sweat rash between my thighs were they had been rubbing for the last couple of hours, and the fact that my boxer shorts were now a new design of thong, and royally rammed up the crack of my arse didn't make the situation any better. My feet were not feeling the love much either, pretty much soaked since we last set off, and my toes and heels were starting to get sore, marching over this bloody terrain. In summary, all was not well at chez Archie.

We'd been stationary for a while now, and was really starting to shiver, a lot of the lads in our column had got their warm kit out and just put it over the top of all that they were wearing, to minimise pratting around. Enough was enough, and me and Jamie had followed suit, it felt so nice, why we hadn't done it earlier is anyone's guess. Looking left and right of me, I could see some of the lads have a crafty fag inside their quilted jackets to cut down on the glare of their cigarettes, you could tell who was taking a drag and when, because the inside of their jackets would glow brighter than normal, if anything it gave them something to do, and maybe even took their mind of their discomfort. Jamie nudged my arm, and pointed up the line, I looked where he was pointing, and I could see a figure making his way down the line, the smokers around me quickly put out their fags through fear of a bollocking. As the figure got closer, we then recognised the shape as Tony, our Platoon Commander.

"Jamie, go fetch Danny please" he asked quietly and rather politely.

"Roger that" Jamie then shuffled off to the rear of our Platoon, where you would find the Platoon Sergeant following up, giving those who were flagging a fatherly kick up the arse.

John arrived with the other two Section Commanders.

"What's going down boss?"

"Hang on" he replied," all will be revealed"

Danny arrived along with Jamie, who resumed his place in the column.

"Right guys" the Boss began "we are about 16km short of Teal; Patrols are pushing forward to get eyes on the settlement to look for bad guys. This will take a while, since the CO wants no surprises when we get there, so you can bet your dollar on Patrols doing a CTR, before telling the old man we can go into town".

A CTR is what we call a Close Target Recce, Patrols would very slowly, and very carefully push their way into Teal, crawling if needs be, to see if there are any Argentine Soldiers defending it. They could even push their luck and even peer through windows to see if they are sheltering from the cold, nothing could be left to chance. They would even sneak around and come in from a different direction to make sure no enemy was there. If they find enemy, and the odds are in our favour, then they would report back to the CO, and he would begin his battle procedure for the battalion, or if the numbers were that few, Patrols could have a shot at the title, and deal with the enemy themselves. But all this takes time, and in this cold, no one is in the mood to sit around with no Bergens or sleeping bags.

"What the Battalion is going to do, is move in as close as 10km and rest up until Patrols make their report" the Boss paused "so get ready to push forward, questions?"

In the darkness, all he saw was shaking heads. He then moved back up the line, and Danny just sat tight for us to move off, and he could count us, and then join on the end. Reluctantly we shedded our warm kit, and got our shit sorted for another 6 kilometres before we rested up. It was now so cold; my leather gloves no longer insulated my hands, and were now just a cold layer around my hands. My feet were not faring much better. But hey, if you can't take a joke Archie boy, you shouldn't have joined.

Everyone started to get to their feet, all you could hear around us was groaning and cursing, and some were not being all that quiet about it. Danny would approach the individuals causing the commotion and I couldn't hear what he said to them, but they were rather reserved after his little visit. We then started the march again, slowly shuffling forward, and I was expecting the guys leading the way to open the pace again, but it never came. The whole pace and mood had now shifted to the task at hand, the capture of Teal Inlet. If the enemy were worth their pay, and as daring as their pilots were, they could have troops out almost as far as we were as roaming security for their commanders in Teal, who knows? They would be in for a nasty shock to come around the corner and see over six hundred cold, wet British troops, just wanting a brew and a fag, and heavily armed coming towards them. The battalion had its business head on now, slow and methodical, we didn't want to run up the backside of Patrols, and at worse, have another friendly fire incident because everyone is on the lookout for Argies.

The pace, as easy as it was, still caused me to sweat like a maniac, since with the exception of drinking some of my water, and scoffing some of my food, my gear remained the same weight, as when we left San Carlos. My feet were really starting to give me some discomfort now, and starting to feel rather raw. I started to think about the possible battle ahead, would I perform? Would we all survive? would we get ambushed in the next gully?, one thing after another. We made our way off some high ground and into what looked like rather a wide valley of sorts, as we got lower, I could see guys up from having trouble with their footing, and before long, we were trudging through bog and surface water again. Everyone was almost at a standstill, and word came down the line that we had a river crossing, great, as if we weren't piss wet through already. When it came to my turn, just as I got ready to skip across, Jamie piped up,

"If you fall over, that will be so funny"

"Shut up, you dick" I retaliated.

I managed to get across soaked from the knees down, not great, but better than being sat in it, since it was now so fucking freezing. Jamie, the tosser, fared about the same. We continued to move forward and as we started to climb out of this valley, we encountered a series of wire cattle fences. We hand railed one for a short while, when everyone stopped. The moon was out, and I could see quite clearly, large groups of troops being led over to other parts of the valley, probably the other companies, but we stayed put. This time, with no waiting around, I dived straight into my barrel bag for the prized quilted jacket, and it was on in a flash, magic! I fished out some chocolate from my smock, and shared it with Jamie. I looked left and right of me; the lads were getting as comfy as possible, pulling out their ponchos and attaching them to the fence, making a very crude bivi site. John came down the line and called our Section in.

"Get yourselves sorted out, we are going to be here for a while, Patrols are on task now, we are just 9km shy of Teal, get as much rest as you can, no white light, smoke if you want, but don't take the piss, and no cooking, understand?"

We nodded, just keen to rest and sort our feet out. Jamie and I used both our ponchos, I attached mine to the fence, and his was used as a ground sheet. Taking all that kit off was like a gift from the gods, as I took my webbing off, I felt like I was going to float away, and it felt so good to be more nimble again, without all that gear on. I wasted no time getting my quilted trousers on, as well as my waterproofs, just as another layer between me and the cold night air. We arranged our bivi with our weapons in the middle, and our webbing acting as a pillow. Having my quilted suit on felt great, and my waterproofs made them windproof. Before I could attempt to get some sleep, I had to change my socks. One foot at a time, should the bad guys come looking for us, I peeled my right boot off, and I slowly peeled off my sock, so I didn't disturb what blisters I may have produced, since having such cold feet for most of the march, they had grown numb, which in turn, could mask any potential blister problems in the early stages. In the dark, I carefully rubbed my hand over my bare foot, to find rather surprisingly only a couple of small blisters, one on the heel, and one on my big toe. On the march here initially in the first part, they felt bloody massive, but now I felt like abit of a fraud. I rang my sock out as much as I could and stuffed it under my right armpit, the aim of which was for my body heat, what there was of it, would eventually dry the sock.

For a few minutes, I massaged my foot back to life, before fetching my dry socks I had stowed inside my barrel bag. With a dry sock now on, I replaced my boot, since I had no trainers with me, and leaving my boots off would be a bad move, because firstly, I couldn't react to an enemy attack very effectively, and secondly, my feet would swell, and getting my boots back on would be torture. Besides, having John catch me without my boots on was my real motivator for keeping them on. I then repeated the same routine with my left foot. Job done. Time to settle down, and try and get some kip. The half frozen ground made sleep pretty much impossible. The cold seeped through my clothing and after a while, I began to shiver, my feet felt like blocks of ice once again. Jamie fared no better, he was of a slighter frame than me, and so I reckoned he felt the cold more. I ended up in the foetal position, facing inwards with my arms folded, trying to preserve as much warmth as I could. Jamie rolled over and adopted the same position, but facing me. He looked at me, and I could make out a grin under his cam creamed face.

"Fancy a cuddle?"

"You are such a knob" I replied.

He sat up and rubbed his hands together, then started routing through his kit for food.

"This was not in the brochure", he stated "I didn't see this on the bloody recruiting poster".

We had no idea how long we would be here, but I had to admit, the Patrols guys were something else. They had walked the same route we had, and there was the CTR to do as well. Good bunch of operators, the more switched on members of the Battalion went to Patrols, since it would be them talking directly to the CO via radio, describing to him what they can see on the target. Integrity and honesty was the name of the game with them guys, since the CO would act according to the information they gave him. I doubt the CO was getting much kip either, planning the potential battle ahead. I started to drift in and out of sleep, the wind had dropped, but the cold remained, I opened one eye, and I could see over Jamie's shoulder, and saw frost setting on Brandon and Kyle's poncho. My breath was even more prominent in the cold air, I could tell Jamie was still alive, because I could see his breath purging from his nostrils. Some of the other guys had given up trying to sleep, and done away with the light discipline, all around our position I could see light glowing under ponchos where they had the kettle on. To heat up hot water and our rations, we were issued a hexamine cooker each. A very crude but effective piece of kit. A small flimsy metal frame that you unfolded to make a cooking hob, inside was a pack of basically what can be described as a box of firelighters, like what you would have for your barbeque, Hexamine tablets. You'd light one and put your mess tin full of water or some of us sported the metal mug that would fit over the top of your water bottle. This would hopefully bring your water to the boil in a matter of minutes, hey presto, hot water. Seeing everyone around me getting hot food and brews on the go, I sat up and thought, fuck it. I got my brew kit and some porridge out of my webbing and got it all on the go. I gave Jamie a shove, he took one look at what I was up to, and quickly looked around for any sign of swift reprisal, and grinned,

"Great idea Batman, John is going to do his nut", chuckling away.

"Don't think so, there's are burner going under his poncho too"

"Gleaming" Jamie grinned.

I think everyone got to a point where slowly freezing to death was not an option, besides, we were out of sight of Teal, and god forbid the Argie patrol who was to crash this tea party. Jamie reached into his webbing and fished out his porridge, placed it next to mine, since Id already assume the title of chef under this poncho. He then grabbed my brew kit and poured in a sachet of hot chocolate into the mug. Just as well we had porridge on the go, with a drop of chocolate in it, and to finish it off, two big sachets of sugar, gorgeous. We took our time eating our porridge, and the brew went back and forth many times between us, we didn't want it to end. Once finished, and our gear packed away, we'd had enough of lying on a freezing cold floor, and emerged from our poncho to get the blood circulating again. I just jogged on the spot for a few minutes, whilst Jamie did a series of jumps, knees to chest, just to warm up. It must have been contagious, everyone got out of their ponchos and did the same, after a while, some got cigarettes on the go and visited other ponchos, shooting the shit, though everyone took their weapons wherever they went, we still had to have some professionalism. We didn't venture too far, no real reason; it was just too cold to be sociable.

"My round" Jamie announced.

He went back under the poncho to get his brew kit fired up. Magic. As I turned I noticed Brandon walking up the line, poking his head into each poncho as he went, clearly talking to the occupants. He pulled up at ours with some news,

"Second battalion tabbed south last night, and are in a serious scrap as we speak about twenty k's south of San Carlos."

He paused and Jamie's head was already outside the poncho, "seriously?"

Brandon nodded, "John told me to spread the word"

"Casualties?" I asked.

"Some" he murmured, "no names yet, I'm sure we will find out soon enough".

Brandon continued on his rounds, and I ducked under the poncho for the hot chocolate. We sipped it in turns in silence. We all knew guys in the other Battalions, both first and second. Our training platoon was split amongst the Battalions when we passed out of training. Casualties, that now made things around here very real, this wasn't just going to be strong talk in Westminster, and we knew the Navy had taken a battering already, but for troops to be in action on the ground this soon, Maggie wasn't fucking around. John poked his head in our poncho, scaring this shit out of us.

"Pack your shit; we are moving now, no one's home"

We looked at him blankly, not too sure how to take the news.

"Patrols have reported back, any Argies that had been there fucked off days ago, and there appears to be none in the area as far as they are concerned, now get ready to move".

He walked off down the line, and we quickly downed the remains of our brew, and started packing our gear in quick time. The frost had really settled on my poncho, to a point that I had to really work the material so I could pack it away in my barrel bag. All over the valley, you could see troops getting packed, ready for the move into Teal. Light began to appear in the east as the sun started to come up and you could see everyone's breath in the cold morning air. I then went through the rigmarole of getting my webbing, ammo, and barrel bag back on my cold, stiff frame for the last push, into Teal that is. Once geared up, we both sat leaning against the fence line, waiting for the order to move out. In the meantime, I thought about our Second Battalion. They must have set off about the same time we did, but clearly on a different route. Was it a deliberate action? Or did they encounter the enemy on their axis of advance. Nothing they couldn't handle I'm sure, but for their battle to still be in full swing was a sobering thought, considering in less than a couple of hours it would be broad daylight. I had professional envy for them, since they had the first bite at the cherry as it were, but to know that they had, and continued to take casualties was something I wasn't in so much of a rush to envy.

Everyone started to get to their feet, everyone groaning like old men getting out of their favourite chair. I hooked my arms over the fence so I could get myself to my feet, but the wire had got caught on my barrel bag, and was now stuck, half squatting against the fence, Jamie just watched and giggled.

"Don't be a dick" I barked and held my hand out for some assistance.

He grabbed my forearm and with his other hand reached behind me to untangle me from the fence. Once free, he helped me upright, and then handed me the gimpy and helmet.

"Here you go mate" he winked.

"Nice one "I replied, "Let's get going, I'm bloody freezing"

Our Platoon started to move off, not entirely sure if we were still in last night's order of march. All around the shallow valley, columns of troops were slowly making their way over to our side as we climbed the gentle gradient , as it levelled out in the far distance, you could see Teal Inlet, the morning sun reflecting off the roofs of the small number of buildings that made up the settlement. If it wasn't for the biting cold, you could mistake it for the mirage of an oasis sat amongst some distant sand dunes. Gimpy on my shoulder, we followed a series of fence lines, since it was as good as daylight now, and since it was revealed there was no enemy in the area, the Battalion slogged it out just to get into Teal as soon as possible. I was soon starting to leak sweat again, since the exertion of the march started to heat up my body under all of my equipment. But this didn't matter; we had ahead of us the potential promise of shelter, hot water, and hopefully somewhere decent to get some kip.

4

Teal Inlet. Not much to write home about if I'm honest, but on this day it had to be one of the best things I had seen for the last couple of days. It was pretty much just a large farm complex, which consisted of the main building, and several smaller houses, along with large sheep sheds, paddocks and pens. The march into Teal was pretty much uneventful. We had covered some gentle rolling moorland, with the odd stream to cross, but nothing outrageous. The lead companies were already in the settlement, snapping up the best spots to bivvy up, but, we had already been given our area to set up shop. As much as the Battalion would love to cram into the buildings in order to get out of the cold, and grab a bed and a bath, this was clearly not going to happen. Besides the fact there wasn't enough room for us all, we were not too far away from enemy forces with a very active air force. Our column came to a halt, and it wasn't long before we were led over to our bivvy area. There was a small cluster of trees at Teal which I found rather bizarre, since we had covered a considerable distance of just bare arsed terrain. These are prime bivvy spots, and the Patrols boys had the monopoly on this real estate, can't say I blame them; they'd been working their arses off since leading us out of San Carlos.

As Jamie and I were sited by Danny, I took a look around, and there were people stood around chatting, getting brews on the go, smoking, and a few others were swinging picks and shovels about, getting their positions sorted. We took off all our gear and, enjoyed the weightlessness for a couple of minutes, before having a stretch off, working out aching shoulders and backs. The weather was starting to close in, and it wouldn't be long before the heavens would open, so Jamie and I broke out the digging tools before we got any cooking on the go. It wasn't long before we were just above shin deep into the ground, and just over knee deep with the spoil built up around three sides of our trench. We left the bottom end of it un spoiled so getting in and out would be easier. The trench was deep enough to get out of the wind, and wide and long enough for us both to lay down when it was time to sleep. We then put Jamie's poncho down as a ground sheet, and used mine as the overhead cover. Being next to a fence line was a nice touch, since fitting my poncho above our trench was made all the more easier. Once complete, it was time to get cooking. Jamie broke out his hexi burner and brew kit, and I rummaged through my webbing for what was left of our rations.

"We should get more rations today" Jamie said as he stirred the brew "and our bergens with abit of luck."

We sat under our poncho while we ate, and the fog was starting to drift into the settlement from the sea, with the fog came a the light spattering of rain on our poncho, nothing heavy, but you could tell it was in for the rest of the day. I wasn't too fuss by this, I had waterproofs, quilted suit, and this would do me ok until I got my bergen back. A pair of boots appeared at the end of our trench, and under the poncho peered Kyle,

"Alright boys? Grab your weapons; the O.C wants to talk to the Company."

We clambered out of our position and followed everyone else who was making their way to the end of our Company line, it wasn't a defensive position as such, and the company was crammed along a series of fence and gorse lines. Most of the company has formed in a big huddle; no one was stood in three ranks, like what would have happened back in Tidworth. I looked around at the guys, we'd been on the islands literally a matter of days, and we all looked like wed been on the Russian Front for a year. We were all filthy, from mud through digging in, sleeping in trenches in just what we were wearing, many of us had dry salt patches on our smocks from the effort of last night's march, all in high spirits, but we just looked like we were in shit state. I peered into the O.C's position, since he had his poncho pitched higher than most, and I could see him chatting away into his radio handset to someone, and in between exchanges, he was sipping on a brew.

"Right listen up fellas," Dale shouted above the din of a Company shooting the shit, we all then became silent.

"The O.C wants to address you guys on events that have taken place since we left San Carlos, after that, 6 Platoon, followed by 5, then 4 with all HQ elements will go over to the main farm building were the lady of the house is dishing out hot chocolate and fried egg sarnies, don't rip the arse out of it, but please go have some, the O.C has been informed that our Bergens will be here by last light, so yes it will be another rummage in the dark for our gear, but we will be sleeping in our bags tonight, fingers crossed. Platoon Sergeants, be ready with a work party to get the rations off the tractors when they arrive, and there will be jerry cans of water available as well. Whilst down at the house, get your water bottles filled there, since it will probably taste better than the sterilized stuff we have, questions?"

No one had any; I think we just had our minds set on fried egg sandwiches. The O.C was now stood next to Dale, who nodded to him and stood to one side.

"Thanks Sergeant Major, gentlemen, I would first like to thank you for your efforts in getting us here, I understand the pace at times was rather tasty, but I'm sure it's nothing you lot can't handle. Our guys that fell out of the march will be arriving with the tractors tonight, so let's make sure they have somewhere to sleep, and they get back into Company routine as soon as possible. No doubt they will be a source of entertainment for some of you, but bear in mind, we start walking again tomorrow, since the C.O is keen to push east as soon as possible, and get eyes on the enemy."

He paused, whilst we looked at each other with a raised eyebrow.

"The Second Battalion, moved South from San Carlos shortly after we moved East yesterday, and are now at the settlement known as Goose Green. It was heavily defended, and a long fight for it took place, which resulted in a large number of casualties, among their dead are their Commanding Officer and their Adjutant"

The fact that he mentioned the word "dead" had us all opened mouthed, never mind the fact that their C.O and Adj had been killed.

"The Regimental Sergeant Major has the casualty list down at the main house, when you go down there later, feel free to look at it, no doubt you will recognise some of the names, since the Battalion have reported fifteen killed and almost fifty wounded. The enemy however, took one hell of a beating, but their dead and wounded have yet to be established, and over a thousand of them were taken prisoner."

He paused; already the guys were a mixture of bowed heads, and smiles and back slapping through Regimental pride.

"In summary gentlemen, we have met the enemy, and they have been found wanting, they are not a match for a professional, fit, and aggressive army such as ours, but don't think they will be a walk over, but give them a bloody nose, they are not so keen for it afterwards, if there are no further questions, enjoy your sandwiches."

We all walked back to our positions, everyone a mixed bag of emotions, sorrow for the guys that had been killed and wounded, proud that the

Regiment had once again shown they are the right guys for the job, but also professional jealousy that the Second Battalion had got their hands dirty first. It was clear now, that we had all, as a nation, gone well past talking our way out of this mess, we were now clearly at war, and I don't think we'd been in it this deep since Korea.

"Weapons and smocks only boys", John came walking down the Section line,"if you've got shaving kits, bring em too".

My shaving kit was in my bergen, not that I needed it in any particular hurry, but I was rather looking forward to brushing my teeth, you know when you have ripped the arse out of it when you can taste your own breath. I picked up the gimpy, and kept the belt of 100 on it, but wrapped it round the body so it didn't swing all over the place. Gun on shoulder, we made our way over to the main building, where cooking was clearly on the go, as smoke billowed constantly out of its chimney. As we got close to the house, I noticed a group of guys stood outside the front door, smoking, and generally just chewing the fat. At first I thought they were the farmers from the settlement, but as I got closer, it was clear that farming was the furthest thing from their mind. Heavily bearded, a mixture of military and civilian ski bobble hats on heads with various lengths of hair. Civilian duvet jackets, that wouldn't look out of place at Everest base camp. Combat trousers, civilian walking boots, and to top off this image, a mixed bag of American weapons, and the odd gimpy for good measure. They looked pretty menacing to me, but that instantly faded, when John shook their hands, and wrapped his arm round one of them and gave him a mock jab on the jaw. I looked over to Davo, and he must have read the look on my face.

"SF" Davo grinned "probably ex-Third Battalion".

This was my first look at our Special Forces, not quite what I had in mind, but they looked like they meant business, despite looking like heavily armed farmers, they clearly had a purpose here, and if I was a betting man, I'd bet they were here at Teal to dish out something nasty in the area. Whilst John was chatting to them, Charlie, our Commanding Officer, came out of the front door, and gathered with the SF guys, after a brief chat, and shaking of hands, the C.O led them into the house, clearly for a more sensitive discussion, and John walked back over to us with a rare grin on his face.

"Haven't seen Kev for years, didn't realise he'd done Selection"

Selection being the notorious course to get into SF. Get into the Parachute Regiment was tasty enough, but Selection was in a league of its own, not for the faint hearted.

We joined the back of the queue, which was filing passed what appeared to be the kitchen window, since I doubt the lady of the house wanted us lot filling through her gaff with muddy boots on. As I got to the window, a lad not much younger than me, probably the son, handed me a lukewarm egg sandwich, and a mug of hot chocolate, that was fucking hot! I nearly dropped it, but I managed a quick regain. I thanked him and behind him I could see what I could only guess were his sister and his mum beavering away with cooking and hot chocolate making, trying to keep up with demand. As we moved around the backside of the house, there was chaos. Troops everywhere most stripped to the waist around oil drums with big bowls of hot water on top, shaving soap plastered all over their faces. I didn't need to strip down, which I was pleased about, since a thick, cold fog had well and truly settled on the settlement. The sandwich was cold by the time a found a spot to put the gun down and tuck in. I wasn't going to complain, since it was either a cold egg sandwich, or dehydrated beef stew from our ration packs. The Hot Chocolate was bang on; I sipped it slowly not wanting to finish it. I slowly took in the scene around me, half naked troops shaving in the freezing fog; the washing line that belonged to the family was overloaded with various items of military clothing, weapons and webbing all over the place. Troops smoking whilst cleaning weapons, some sorting their feet out, troops nearer the house were digging trenches. Teal was really a mixed bag of activity. Through the thick fog, out in the bay you could just make out shipping that had arrived, probably loaded with stores and all sorts of nasty stuff to fight the bad guys with. Bearing in mind I had not even seen an Argentine soldier yet, but I'm sure it wouldn't be long, one way or the other.

"Platoon Sergeants to me!" Dale yelled over the din of troops milling about, shooting the shit. Everyone quietened down, probably intending to eavesdrop on Dales talk with Danny and the other Sergeants. They were too far away to make out what they were saying, but judging by the Sergeants scribbling furiously into their notebooks as Dale dictated, something was on the cards. They then dispersed and the Sergeants, including Danny called for their platoons to gather around them. In less than a minute, in whatever state of dress or stage of shaving people were in, everyone was in their relevant huddle to receive the information. Danny waited patiently for us all to get into a spot so we could see and hear him clearly.

"Guys, Second Battalion's casualty list, only the dead at this time, but I'm sure word about the wounded will be around soon enough."

He had everyone's undivided attention, as he read the names, slowly and deliberately. Now and again as he read out the full title of the soldiers killed at Goose Green, as in Rank, and full name, someone gave a low whistle, or cursed under their breath. You could tell by some of the guy's reactions that they clearly knew these men, either through work, socially, or long time friends. You could have knocked us over with a feather, because it's not until they read the name out, does the whole magnitude of what has taken place really sinks in. We are at war, we are killing each other, and it is not an exercise. I recognised one of the names, a Corporal that was my training NCO in Aldershot. To us he was harsh but fair, proud of his Regiment, and would do anything to preserve its reputation, and god forbid anyone that had another opinion about it that wasn't to his liking. He was my instructor, I never really chatted to him, certainly never drank with him, apart from when my folks attended my Pass Out parade at the end of training. In the NAAFI, which is basically a forces social club he came over to where me and my parents were stood having a beer, and he chinked my glass with his, and informed my parents that I wasn't a bad kid, and should do ok in Battalion, and with that he walked off on his rounds chatting to other parents. I had no real emotion over his death, in fact felt rather at peace knowing that he had died in a matter that was probably to his liking and wondered what happened to the Argentine soldier that had a hand in his death.

Danny snapped us out of it.

"Lads, the Boss and O.C are in with the C.O. with regards to our possible move east tonight, not sure when we will see our bergens, but things are starting to heat up, and I'm not talking about the weather."

He had a point, with this fog in, it was bloody freezing.

"Get your shit together, and get ready for another long night, I will get more information to you as I find out more, crack on."

With that, we dispersed, all heading back to our ponchos, the main thing on my mind was getting abit of rest before we started tabbing again. Just as we got back to our positions, I could hear engine noise getting louder from the west side of the settlement, and as it grew louder, an annoying creaking and rattling of metal. It was catching the attention of everyone around me, and it briefly crossed my mind that armoured vehicles were coming into town, whose was anyone's guess.

"Tractors are here", someone called out. The nervous suspense subsided instantly as a long column of tractors and trailers arrived alongside the main settlement house. Trailers brimming with bergens, with a few guys sat on top, tractors dragging pallets with missiles, and all sorts of ammo wrapped in cargo netting. One trailer was straining under the weight of tons of rations in their brown cardboard boxes. Other tractors had trailers brimming with all sorts of randomness, but all I was interested in right now was the rations and my bergen. Without being prompted guys began to unload the bergens, placing them into Company lines for their owners to collect when allowed. The tractors dragging all the ammo was led down towards the water's edge away from the buildings, I take it so if Ayrton and his boys paid us a visit, we would not all go up in a colossal explosion of stacked ammunition, good job the fog was in to be fair. The ration trailer was being parked alongside a barn of sorts, and the guys formed a human chain, lugging to each other, emptying the trailer in quick time.

The hive of activity soon petered out, and I took the chance to grab my bergen, and after a few minutes scrabbling through what was left of our Company kit, I found it. As I got back to my poncho, Jamie was sat outside it squaring his feet away. Leighton and Kyle, along with Davo were coming down the line dropping off four boxes of 24hr rations and a couple of packets of the hexamine fuel at each poncho, so that was one less chore to do. Zane came over puffing and panting with two full jerry cans of water, which he placed down next to us, so if anyone wanting to fill water bottles they didn't have to travel far, because our poncho was in the middle of our Section position. John was nowhere to be seen, someone had called for all Section Commanders whilst the tractors were being unloaded. No doubt he was being briefed up on tonight's activities. Once Id sorted my feet out, powdered, fresh socks, and my beloved trainers on, I felt like a new man. I thought I'd better give the Gimpy abit of care and attention. By rights what should happen is Weapon, Kit, Self, but I was already halfway through sorting my feet out, when I noticed some of the guys stripping and cleaning their weapons. The gun only needed a quick spruce, bearing in mind I hadn't fired the thing since we got ashore, apart from a little bit of rust here and there which I quickly dealt with, using one of the wire brushes in my cleaning kit, she was good to go. A quick lick of oil on the working parts, Robert is your mothers' brother.

Jamie and I then broke open the new rations and squeezed them into our webbing and the goodies went back in the smock pockets for quick access during the tab. Once our gear was sorted, we stowed all our gear, including our bergens under the poncho. The cardboard from the ration packs, we flat packed them and lined the bottom of our position for a bit of insulation from the cold earth under Jamie's poncho. After rearranging our kit a few times, like moving furniture around a small room, we then got the kettle on, for a well earned cup of tea. We'd just brewed up and got comfy when Davo stuck his head under the poncho.

"Boss is back, just come as you are."

We clambered out and the Boss, along with John was stood a little away from the ponchos. We all gather around them, as the remainder of the Platoon was rounded up by Danny. After a couple of feet stamping minutes in the cold fog filled air, everyone had assembled.

"Guys" the Boss began, "the Commanding Officer is keen for us to march east to a settlement called Estancia tonight, 26 K's away."

There was a few sighs, but business was business. He continued.

"SF has put any move east out of bounds until at least 0600 hours tomorrow, because they have some business to take care of first that will make our move to Estancia free of enemy. So as it stands we will be stopping here tonight, and now we have our bergens, life will be a little more comfortable, at least for tonight. Patrols are to move off East at 0615, and once they have established a suitable lead, we will then move off. Bergens will stay here again, and the tractors will follow on with them later. Questions?"

There were none, as the boss walked off, me and Jamie high fived, and got back under the poncho, and wrestled with our bergens, forcing them to give up their precious booty called sleeping bags.

Once all snug in my bag, I was rather relieved that we were not pushing forward tonight, since sleep was on my list of priorities. Besides, SF had some business to take care of and far be it for me to rush them. I drifted in and out of sleep as the evening wore on, due to the fact that there was still a lot of activity going on around the settlement, tractors moving about, people calling out for the lads to come and collect their bergens etc.

Sometime later, I felt my shoulder being given a shove.

"Mate, here you go."

I rolled over, and Jamie was handing me food and brew. I sat up with my head brushing the underside of the poncho. Once I managed to focus abit better, I accepted breakfast in bed.

"What time is it?"

"Half Six" he replied "you slept straight through"

I rested my head back on my webbing, and gave out an almighty stretch, a whole night's kip without any guard duty. How did that happen?, clearly Jamie didn't get pinged for one either, because he would of put my name on the list for good measure or would of dragged me out of bed to keep him company for that cold hour or so. I propped myself up abit more so I could eat and drink without wearing half of it. It was very cold this morning, our breath very prominent in the air under our poncho. Jamie was still in his bag eating away at a leisurely pace, watching the world go by. Not that there were much of a world going by at this time. There were a few people moving about, tractors could be heard moving about behind us, and the odd helicopter zooming about, but nothing to get excited about.

As I took in more of the sweet tea Jamie had lovingly prepared, I noticed a pair of legs arrive at Jamie's side of the poncho. Davo knelt down, and with a grin he rested on his side and helped himself to Jamie's cup of tea.

"Listen up lads, the Commandos will be arriving shortly, and we need to make room for them. Patrols left some time ago and have now established themselves some distance away to the East towards Estancia House. We will be leaving in a little while, so get your gear together, more details to follow, ok?"

With that he left, I didn't want to get out of my bag, since it was bloody freezing outside, but orders were orders, and we had business of our own to take care of. Once breakfast was finished, we forced ourselves out of our bags and into our quilted suits in record time. We already knew we wouldn't be taking bergens again for this move, so our packing routine was pretty much the same as when we tabbed out of San Carlos. Once packed away, including our ponchos, we both sat on our bergens in front of our hole with our marching kit placed in front of us. Looking left and right, others had pretty much done the same. A light fog hung in the air, so therefore you couldn't see the whole settlement. Out in the bay, I could just make out the outline of a ship or two, I just hoped the Argy Air force wasn't knocking about, and had noticed them, or else this morning was going to be a repeat of San Carlos the other day. People started shouting up the line about bergens to be taken over to Dale's position, and with smocks and weapons only, we did just that. We hung around by the bergen stack, shooting the shit with a few of the guys we hadn't seen for a couple of days, when one of them pointed out a rather bizarre sight on the outskirts of the settlement. In the light fog, appeared what I thought was livestock wandering in between the buildings. Very quickly it was clear that these huge lumbering beasts were in fact human beings. As they drew closer, you could make out weapons in their hands and Green berets on, the Commandos had arrived. They looked completely shattered, the lead one stopped moving and leant back slumping to the floor, a few of our lads ran over to help him. The other marines lined up behind him did the same, with our guys helping loosen their bergen straps. They must have walked the whole route so far, with bergens. More staggered into Teal, very tired, it was clear this was maybe the Commandos we encountered on the way out of San Carlos, and had moved north. They got themselves sorted out into Company lines, and removed their bergens, and went straight into admin, sorting their feet out, a few just sat on the ground, enjoying a cigarette.

"Right, shows over, let them get themselves sorted" Dale shouted "get back to your positions and get ready to move."

As we walked back to our positions, I don't think I heard anyone take the piss out of the commandos, since such an opportunity is rarely allowed to go to waste, but seeing them stagger into the settlement with all that kit on, maybe humbled a few of us. The Commandos were tough, make no mistake, I think we just appreciated the fact that our Commanding Officer wanted his Paratroopers to move quick and light, even if it meant being colder as a result.

"Kit on" Danny shouted out" follow me"

With all my kit on once again, I shuffled it about so it would sit comfortably for the march ahead, and with helmet on, and Gimpy on my shoulder I followed Jamie and the rest of the Platoon to the eastern side of the settlement where the Company was gathering. Leaning on a fence in the Company location, we could see the Commandos taking up residence in our previous trenches, one less thing for them to do before they get in their sleeping bags I suppose. Slowly but surely, the Battalion began its march East once again, en route to a settlement called Estancia House, 26 kilometres away.

5

It wasn't long before a cracking pace was set again, and I was sweating like a maniac, with gun on shoulder trying to keep up. The terrain hadn't changed, long uphill gradients, low boggy grass, numerous river crossings, ankle deep tussock grass, which really gave your feet some stick. Every hour we stopped for a few minutes, before setting off again. At one particular rest stop, I noticed the mountain ranges were starting to appear. On HMS Intrepid, we had a series of briefs about the layout of the islands, and that their capital Port Stanley was surrounded by mountains, so I guess we weren't that far from there. I'm not sure if it was due to my sweat cooling when we rested, but it really was starting to get colder. We set off again, two columns of troops stretching out ahead of me, everyone fighting their own loads, the radio operators with their bergens, struggling to keep up with their rather energetic commanders. I was content with my lot in life right now, just a gunner lumbering along, with Jamie as my ammo donkey.

It was starting to get dark when we stopped again. Danny and John came up the line letting us know that Patrols were now checking out Estancia, but early reports showed that there were no enemy there, result; I wasn't in the mood for a scrap right now. Same routine as before, we got as comfy as possible, waiting for Patrols to give us the nod to move into the Settlement. Quilted suit and fresh socks on, Jamie and I got a Hot Chocolate on the go, and just talked about random shit as it presented itself. Some of the lads had found a fence line to set up their ponchos, and try and get some kip, but it was far too cold for that. We chose to just sit there and keep warm with brews. Danny and the boss came up the line and called the Platoon together. Jamie was dispatched by Danny to turf the guys out from their ponchos, which was not the most popular task in the world, but ignore Jamie at your peril, because the following wakeup call would be by Danny, and with his own method of swift justice. We had all gathered.

"Guys" the Boss began "we are now very much on the enemy's doorstep. Estancia is clear for us, so we will be moving shortly. Same drill as before when we get there, but as before, don't expect a long stay. There will be no more lounging around, as we did in Teal, we will almost be on the FLET, and with this is the possibility of counter attack, any questions?"

There were none.

With that they moved back to their places in the march. The FLET means Forward Line of Enemy Troops, basically the front of the enemy positions, which meant at anytime from here on in, there was a real chance of encountering the enemy carrying out their patrols.

The cold was really getting to us now, as we waited for the Company to head off on the last stretch into the settlement. The column then started to shuffle forward, and believe it or not, it was rather nice to get back into our usual tabbing stride, since this kept the cold at bay until our next rest stop. Off to our right side as we moved into the settlement was the beginning of a large series of hills, and I hoped the enemy wasn't watching our every move as we slogged along with all this kit on. Then I remembered the Boss saying something about SF making sure our move would be enemy free when they had finished a particular task they were undertaking, I just hoped they got it done before we showed up.

We got into Estancia in the early hours, and were very quickly guided into our areas by the lads from patrols, Battalion Headquarters once again had set up shop in the main building, lucky for them, and as usual, us Company peasants got given a fence line to pitch our ponchos on. We got put into position by Danny, who said for us to rest up, no briefs to be had as of yet, so maximum rest, no fucking about. Jamie and I went about our usual routine, shelter sorted, quilted suits on, then quick inspection of our feet. Mine were not looking too clever, the constant wet and increasing cold from that last march had my feet looking like I'd spent too long in the bath. I made sure I gave them a good foot rub before I put dry socks on, bearing in mind I only had clean ones in my bergen, but dry all the same. Once this done, I settled down on Jamie's freezing cold poncho. I was tired, but sleep was impossible, it was just too damn cold. At this point, I was noticing that my lower back and hips were very sore, partly due to weight loss perhaps, but also from my webbing belt. The canvas material, when wet begins to shrink slightly and become less flexible, resulting in webbing sores. Not much I could do about it right now, besides, I'm sure there were a lot of the guys nursing similar injuries if not worse. There were a few of the guys hiding injuries, such as turned ankles from the initial march out of San Carlos, but not letting on. The pride of some people. I drifted in and out of sleep, but whenever I woke I would shiver like mad and try and tuck in closer to Jamie, not that he was any better off, in fact he was probably colder than me, since I had more meat on the bone shall we say, and he was built like a jockeys whip.

"I'm not easy you know", he mumbled through his hood.

"What?"

"You haven't even bought me a drink, and you're trying your luck"

Comedy is all about timing, so I'm told, and Jamie always had time for it. I wanted a brew, but couldn't face having cold air whipping around under my armpits where I managed to retain some heat. I caught the aroma of tobacco, and burnt matches; someone had clearly given up on the "sleep in a freezer" competition, and got a fag on the go. I rolled over onto a cold patch of ground and saw numerous people laying under their ponchos with fags on the go, or stood up outside theirs, smoking their heads off, and stamping their feet. Being a non smoker, I didn't understand the morale aspect of having cigarettes in such circumstances, I'd smoked in training, but only because I thought it looked hard, but when I got to Battalion, it just faded away like many of the hobbies I'd under taken in my youth. I could hear more people moving about, the clatter of mess tins, a random heavy cough from under a poncho, numerous farts, the usual dawn chorus of soldiers trying to come to life in a frozen farmer's field. I rolled over to face Jamie, but all I was welcomed with was his left hand inside his hood, at which point it produced the hugest bogey I'd ever seen.

"You are such a charmer" I giggled.

"It's got to be your turn to do breakfast" he stated under the hood.

I forced myself to sit up and shift around to get at my webbing. I dug out the gear required for such a feast and got the water on the go. Jamie now sat up, hood still up, and he then scrambled out of his side of the poncho, probably for a morning piss. With water coming to the boil, I sorted us a big sweet cup of coffee and bacon grill. The sun had started to rise at this stage and I became more aware of what was around us. Clambering out of the poncho for a big stretch, I looked around and the settlement which appeared a lot smaller than Teal, was just overwhelmed by ponchos pitched up all over the place. For a professional army, we looked more like a refugee camp. Someone had already found time to exploit the main building washing line, with a random collection of socks and underwear hanging from it, and judging by the condition of those items, they definitely belonged to soldiers. Some guys braved the elements and were stripped to the waist shaving, I rubbed my hand over my own face, and it was clearly evident I would need to carry out the same ablution once my bergen caught up with us. I noticed a huge pile of cubed peat stacked up outside of the main building, with some of the lads taking the odd cube and putting them into the few stoves available in the courtyard.

I noticed Danny walking up the Platoon line, telling the boys to get up and get squared away. As he got to ours, he seemed happy that at least some of his soldiers were up and moving.

"Don't wander too far; the Boss is in with the O.C with regards to our next move."

With that he walked on. Next move? Did this mean we had another tab coming up? Or just what was going to be happening around here? I wasn't feeling the love for another tab just yet, I just wanted my bergen, a shave, fresh socks, and a nice, long, warm kip, and in that order too. There wasn't much to do now, other than wait for the Boss's orders, and our bergens. At this time my stomach turned over, which announced that it was time for me to do something about it. I quickly rummaged through my kit, and found some toilet paper. I grabbed the gimpy and made off to the main building for my call of nature. It was a long shot, but the worse they could say was no. I made my way to the door at the rear of the building, since I'm sure the lady of the house wouldn't appreciate Archie from Portsmouth bounding in through the main door asking for the shitter. I knocked on the door which led directly to the kitchen, but no one responded, so I took a chance and slowly opened the door. As I peered through the gap, I could see a lot of people including our O.C, and the heavily armed farmers from Hereford pouring over a map on the kitchen table.

"Can we help you mate?" said a voice to my right, giving me such a fright, my package almost made a premature appearance.

I looked round, and one of the SF guys was leaning against the door frame with a radio handset to his ear. I made my pathetic plight to him,

"Erm, toilet?"

"Front door mate, now piss off!"

Door shut, I made my way around to the front door, calling myself a dickhead for representing myself and my Regiment in such a poor light, like a scruffy orphan asking for the scraps from the masters table. I know approached the main door with less caution, and even though I knocked, I made my way in. The house was a hive of activity, officers pouring over maps, signallers listening intently to radio traffic, the lady of the house with a tray of hot drinks doing the rounds. I managed to make eye contact with her, and he looked me up and door, smiled as she shook her head and indicated with a head jerk and a raised eyebrow clearly the room I was after, the toilet. I locked myself in and stripped off all my warm kit, and parked my arse on the cool, clean throne. Priceless.

I finished what needed to be done and made sure I cleaned up after myself, not wanting this gift from the gods to be removed from us due to the odd soldier not respecting the facility. As I made my way to the front door, the lady, whom I never got to speak to or even thank properly gave me a thumbs up as I left. Thank you. As I got back to my poncho, no one was around, and then it suddenly dawned on me that I'd disobeyed Danny, fear and dread filled me instantly, you don't ignore Danny.

"Archie"

I spin on my heels and saw Jamie waving me over to where the whole Platoon was gathered around the Boss's poncho. I dashed over and plonked my arse down next to Jamie, not wanting to make eye contact with anyone. No such luck, as I glanced up Danny was glaring straight at me, and in an attempt to break his gaze I looked over to John who was glaring at me just as intense. Not good, John had clearly received a bollocking from Danny, and this was not going to end well for me. I looked for comfort in the eyes of my Platoon Commander, but he didn't appear in the mood for entertaining me either.

"Now that we are now all together, I will cover the details again for young Archie's benefit"

Mutterings of "prick" and "crow" were heard amongst the audience as I looked at the ground for inspiration. At our feet was the Boss's map and he had a pencil in his hand to point out various points during his delivery.

"To orientate you to the map, this is where we are now, Estancia, and if you look over your right shoulder you will see the summit of Mount Kent, which is here."

Sorted, I'm happy where we are, please get on with it. He continued.

"SF and Commandos with the only remaining Chinook took a daring bound forward the other night and seized this vital feature from the enemy, after a brief but heavy contact, the enemy withdrew and we now control the high ground overlooking our current position, hence the reason our move here was delayed, the last thing we need is to have our position under observation and the threat of air and artillery attack."

He paused to let it sink in.

"Further to that, SF also destroyed a small garrison of enemy troops at a place called Top Malo House, which left untended, could have given us trouble from the right as we moved here, and could also mount raids against us while we catch our breath."

He then pointed to the high ground on the map and also where it was on the ground.

"These features here now hide us from view from the enemy defences around Port Stanley, Mount Estancia here, and Mount Vernet here. Once over the skyline of these features, we will be in full view of the enemy, and also their Artillery foot print. Patrols Company will be pushing into No-Man's Land tonight to establish a patrol base at a place called Murrell Bridge and from there will receive CTR tasks for our next objectives, any questions?"

"Fighting patrols?" John asked.

"Most likely", replied the Boss, "we have to ensure our patrol programme doesn't clash with what the Commandos have in mind, and the C.O is keen for us not to have a repeat of what happened at San Carlos. Once Patrols have established our battle space and objectives, we will then build our patrol programme, any other questions?"

No more questions.

"Right then guys, it's the real deal, we've got business to take care of, the C.O wanted the Battalion to advance to contact all the way into Stanley, but Brigade said no, as they want a Brigade action to take place shortly, just waiting for all the right pieces to get into place before we kick off. If there are no more questions, get yourselves tidied up, and our bergens should be here shortly."

Everyone started to disperse, but Danny pointed at me and summoned me over. Sheepishly, I approached him, John came over as well.

"Do I speak another language to you do I?" demanded Danny.

"No Sergeant", I replied, awaiting my fate.

"Drop the Sergeant shit, you know that's not how I roll, don't mug me off you little dickhead, or else the Argentines will be the least of your problems, do you understand me?"

"Yes Danny"

"Right then, when the tractors arrive, I hope you're feeling strong, because you are on bergen detail, and my shit list for the rest of the day, so any poxy jobs need doing, you are on the top of my list, understand?"

I nodded.

"Besides, how the hell did you blag using the bogs in the house? I went to use them, and some twat of an officer told me to go away".

I grinned "my boyish charms".

"Well they haven't helped you in this case have they? Now piss off".

I legged it back to my position before I pushed my luck too far. Jamie was getting the kettle on as I arrived. I mulled a few things over as we waited for the water to boil. Things were getting serious, since the Boss was talking about things like "battle space" and "fighting patrols". From what I could gather, battle space was an area of ground that the Battalion could operate without, in theory, other units coming into, since they would have their own battle space, and hopefully this would prevent friendly fire incidents, since we tend to do most of our business in the dark, so clarity is important. As for "fighting patrols", I was more familiar with these, you go out in no less than platoon strength, so you are looking at least thirty plus troops, and deliberately pick a fight with the enemy, giving them a bloody nose, lowering their morale, so their patrols, if any would take place, would not be effective, and therefore you dominate No-Man's Land. That term in itself, seemed rather surreal, I couldn't help but think about the Somme and the stretch of land between the trenches. The same principle applies, but more land between them and us.

Jamie snapped me out of it. "What did he say?"

"I'm on his shit list, at least for the day."

"Don't be getting me roped into your unfortunate business" he stated "I'm getting my bergen, and getting my fat head right down."

"Don't be like that, besides many hands make light work and all that."

"Piss off, drink your brew." It seemed that everyone was telling me to jog on today.

It wasn't long before the tractors came rattling and squeaking into town, so without waiting to be reminded, I got my weapon slung and in just my smock began to make my way over to the main building.

"Archie", John hollered, "take that skinny gob shite with you; you will only get lonely otherwise."

With great delight, I jogged back to our poncho to turf Jamie out.

"You are such a wanker", he mumbled under his breath, "and him" indicating John.

"Come on, we get first dibs on our own kit while we are there".

Same as before when they got to Teal, the ammo tractors were led well away from where we were all kipping and the buildings. Bergens were sorted in next to no time, and as we found our Platoons kit we put it to one side. Brandon and Zane took our kit back to our poncho for us. Then the rations got dumped in a sheep shed along with any other weird and wonderful stuff that had made its way onto the trailers. We got a sweat on, but knowing we were merely minutes away from fresh socks and dry, warm sleeping bags made it a worthwhile effort.

Returning to our position, admin was very much the order of the day, and every appeared to be enjoying having their bergens back in their grubby mitts. I wasted no time getting my act together since I'm sure Danny had more shit jobs for me to do during the course of the day, so I needed to be quick and get some down time in the green maggot. Feet, done and dusted with fresh socks on in record time, with trainers on. Straight away, ask any soldier, fresh socks on in any part of the world, you do feel like a new man. Then came the shave, some different schools of thought over this ablution, some go hardcore, and go for the cold water option. I'm a big fan of this if the weather is favourable, but at Estancia House, with a freezing fog creeping in from the sea, I'm going the extra mile and boiling some water for this. Water on the go, I dig deep into my bergen, and fish out my shaving kit. Into the mess tin of water goes my razor and shaving brush. Once the water is hot enough, in goes the flannel and I'm on my way. A hot water shave is a lovely experience when you are in a cold place, Estancia more than qualifies. Once the shave was over, I peered about and couldn't see anyone rushing to get more cam cream back on, so I thought I'd leave it to a more relevant time. Next on my to-do list is the Gimpy, not that she really needed it, so I gave her a quick wipe down and oiling, but what I did take my time on, was the belts of ammo that had been draped over me for some time. I gave them a thorough wipe down and carefully inspected them for rust. Once done I then filled my water bottles from my webbing as the jerry can was once again in the middle of the Section line next to our poncho. No more rations to dish out just yet since wed been restocked at Teal. All done.

Just as I was getting myself ready for bed, another bombshell hit our ears, not just mine.

"Dig in" Danny shouted up the line.

"Bollocks" I cursed under my breath, trying not to get overwhelmed with anger. I should have seen this coming. From a tactical point of view, this should have been the first thing we addressed, but I suppose these things happen in war. Fuck it, get on with it. Jamie was grinning at me as he pulled back my poncho and peeled his off the floor.

"What are you grinning at you dick?" I growled.

"Your face is a picture" he chuckled," I could see you all set for bed and then Wham!"

I was raging, nothing worse than a sudden change of plan. I'm not the best soldier on the planet, but I do like routine, and just when you're in your groove, there is a sudden change, it feels like the worse thing in the world, heaven knows why I joined the Army, the term "Military Precision" was thought up by someone who has never done a day in the military, and that term "remain flexible" is just an officers phrase meaning they haven't got a clue what the fuck is going on. It's a good job I'm paired up with Jamie, because he takes the sting out of any shit situation, and as I calmed down, I did start to see the funny side of things. It wasn't long before our earth works was complete and we set about getting all comfy again. Now in my sleeping bag, the last couple of hours didn't seem all that bad. Jamie got a brew on the go whilst sat up in his bag and gave me the best Hot Chocolate I've ever tasted. I love that guy, but I would never tell him, his head wouldn't fit under our poncho.

6

I woke with a start, fearing I'd missed another briefing by the Boss or Danny, as I looked left and right in the fading light, I could just see guys asleep under their ponchos, or stood about smoking and chatting. I leaned over, and could see Jamie was out for the count, so I just rest my head back on my webbing and looked at the underside of the poncho above our heads. My breath in the cold, foggy air was now very prominent and the poncho had started to frost up. Why the guys were stood around chatting and stamping their feet was beyond me, since I'd have taken refuge in a sleeping bag hours ago. I looked at my watch; I'd certainly pushed out a few hours, with not so much of a shove from Danny with regards to my cock up earlier on. Danny was an okay guy, he wasn't one of them seniors that screamed and shouted, trying to shove everything Airborne down your throat, don't get me wrong, he was proud of his Regiment, but he was a good operator, and did the job the way it should be done, either full on, or not at all. When Danny tears a strip off you, it's not a frenzied, spit flying rage, since troops get immune to that, and after a while it becomes a source of entertainment. The way Danny makes you feel like a turd is by acting like a disappointed father, and that cuts me to the core better than any scream fit.

I just lay there planning world domination in my head when I noticed John making his way up the line, stopping at every poncho on the way up, and peering underneath. I could hear muffled chat, but couldn't make out what was being said, I felt at ease that it wasn't a shit job from Danny on its way to me, since John knew exactly where I was sleeping, and would have come straight to me. Once he finished chatting with Kyle and Zane, he then moved over to us, as he arrived, I propped myself up on my right elbow to receive whatever was coming. As he knelt down, he pulled back Jamie's hood on his sleeping bag, Jamie jumped out of his skin.

"Relax, you idiot" John grinned, something was up, John was gentle and smiling.

"Guys, just to keep you in the picture, Patrols have now moved out towards Murrell Bridge to establish a patrol base in that area. Our objective has been selected for us, it's a feature called Longdon."

He paused, allowing it to slowly seep into our heads.

"Patrols will begin to CTR Longdon once they have established themselves at Murrell, more info to follow, any questions?"

As usual, none.

Without ceremony, he stood up, and moved onto the next position. I lay back down with not much to think about except the fact that we were looking at attacking this Longdon place pretty soon. I hadn't written home since we got here, mainly to do with being pretty busy in the last few days, and so far, with the exception of the air attacks at San Carlos, everything we'd done was not any different than any exercise I'd done. Tabbing, sweating, shivering, sleeping, eating, the usual stuff. I leant over to Jamie.

"Do you think we will be attacking Longdon soon?" I asked.

"Mate, Patrols will take their time checking that place out before we go anywhere; we are going to be here for a while".

He had a point, if the recce of Teal was anything to go by, the Patrol guys do like to take their time, and the last thing I wanted to do right now is rush them. They would go out of their way to ensure every enemy position is noted, since the last thing we needed was to encounter positions unmarked, since that could spell disaster in any attack. Take your time guys, take your time. The remainder of the night went without incident, but at one point, I'm sure I heard machine gun fire out in No-Man's Land.

I came to at first light, and Jamie was sat up getting his quilted suit on.

"Get up mate, the Boss wants to talk to us."

I lay back on my webbing, wishing the Boss would do a door to door information service like John did last night. I got myself out of my bag and into my quilted gear, since it was very cold this morning, and I noticed Danny was calling for us all to come as we are. Without waiting for him to get impatient, we jogged over to the Boss's poncho, we all gathered round, not wanting to sit on the frozen ground, so the Boss chose to stand when addressing us.

"Guys, Patrols made contact with the enemy last night, in the area of Murrell Bridge. After a brief but fierce firefight, they managed to beat the enemy back and they withdrew in the direction of Mount Longdon. Patrols followed up with the intention of grabbing any enemy that were wounded in the exchange, but the enemy didn't hang around."

Blimey, this shit was really happening now. He continued.

"No casualties suffered by our guys, thankfully. Patrols are staying at Murrell in order for us to dominate No-Man's Land, and conduct operations from there. Pretty soon, they will have established our battle space, and then we can also patrol out there, and getting a feel for the ground ahead. Behind the main building is an area taped off. No one is to go in there, since some of the Patrols guys will be coming back with information to build a model for the up and coming operations. More info will follow as we receive it. The C.O also wants the companies to push out onto Mounts Vernet and Estancia so we can get eyes on the objective, Mount Longdon. Any questions?"

"When do we move up the hill?" John asked.

"No time has been given yet, as said before, more info to follow."

John nodded with satisfaction.

"Right guys" the boss continued," it's very much a waiting game for the time being, just keep yourselves busy and you gear squared away, things could change very rapidly, and we may need to act fast, speak to you later."

We made our way back to our positions, feeling at a bit of a loose end. Our admin was all done, we literally had not much to do, we couldn't check fire our weapons, since that would blatantly advertise our location, so it was very much a case of twiddling our thumbs for the time being.

Over the next few days, things began to develop with regards to our mission. Guys from Patrols would move back to Estancia for rest and also to begin construction of the earth model which would be used to deliver orders for the operation. Earth models are usually referred to as the Private soldiers map, since its normally just the commanders, ranging from Lance-Corporal and above that possess maps and compasses, and if us Privates can see what the mission will entail, then we have a better understand of what is required of us. The Patrols lads didn't spoil the area marked off for them with any digging, they brought in spoil from somewhere else in the settlement and began to sculpt whatever it was they were trying to build. In its early stages, it was nothing more than just random piles of spoil all over the shop, and then a few days later, those piles were actually shaped to represent what was actually out in No-Man's Land. Then they had one big pile of spoil off the right of the smaller piles, and it then dawned on me what was taking place. The smaller piles were the area in general, by that I mean, not just Longdon, but the surrounding features as well, and the big pile of spoil was Longdon in detail. Slowly but surely, more meat was being added to the bone.

Other members of the Battalion began patrolling out to our front, in order to build a better picture of what was out there, there was some Company activity out there, but I was not part of them patrols, the aim of which was to recce sites for fire support teams with their machine guns, and MILAN anti-tank systems. MILAN was a Belgian designed anti-tank system that fired missiles on a wire and the firer could control the missile by keeping the crosshairs on the target and a pulse signal was sent down the wire which commanded the missile to move up and down, left and right. The enemy didn't have any armoured vehicles as far as we knew, so it was decided they would be used to smash any bunkers or strong points we encountered. Snipers also moved out to our front with Patrols, and would loiter out there, reporting on what they observed, and kill key personnel if the opportunity arose. Key personnel would include, Commanders, anyone that could be seen to be in charge, and to the trained eye, your body language could give away the fact that you was a leader or not. Radio operators, the antenna sticking out of your back pack made you Sniper bait. Machine gunners, shoot them and the enemy has no heavy firepower, and the ultimate prize for any Sniper, enemy Snipers, deal with them, and you have the enemy laid out before you like a buffet. You are spoilt for whom to shoot first.

"Listen up guys" Danny bellows," make your way over to the main building in five minutes for orders, I'm sure Archie can squeeze in a quick shit in that time."

He winked at me, he hadn't forgotten.

I grinned and took it on the chin. What does a man have to do to make amends? Word got around quickly that we only needed to take weapons with us and to bring brews if we wanted, since we could be a while. Jamie was already putting the finishing touches to a couple of Hot Chocolates when it was time to go over to the house.

"Nice one matey" as I gratefully received a cup.

The whole Platoon made its way over to the house mob handed. As we arrived we were told to hang tight whilst Dale organised who was to sit where. When delivering orders around a model, ideally you want the guys sat in their formations for the operation so they can orientate themselves to the ground, and face the model in the direction they will be travelling. They was abit of shuffling around, Dale putting bums on seats so to speak whilst Justin, our O.C was putting the finishing touches to the notes in his hand. I noticed a few new faces in the audience; probably guys attached to the Company such as Mortar Fire Controllers, Artillery observers etc, anyone that put the cards in our favour when the shooting started. Before long, everyone was in position, and Dale commanded everyone to settle down. I noticed that names of features were now in place on the model on large pieces of card so everyone could read them. Dale stood off to one side with a long stick and handed the orders over to Justin.

"Thank you Sergeant Major, Gentlemen, you are about to receive orders for a deliberate silent Battalion night attack onto Mount Longdon." He paused to allow his bold statement to sink in. We were going in cold, dark, and as quite as possible in order to get on top of the enemy before they reacted.

"Task organisation, B Company complete, attached to us are Mortar Fire Controllers from our Mortar Platoon, Artillery Observers from 29 Commando Royal Artillery, plus Naval Gunfire Observers from HMS Avenger, and Engineers from 9 Squadron, welcome."

So that's who the new faces were. Justin then introduced the model, with Dale pointing out features with the stick he was holding.

"North pointer to orientate you and here you have the area in general. We are here at Estancia House. These piles of spoil are as follows, our objective, Longdon, and these are Wireless Ridge, Tumbledown, Harriet, Two Sisters, William, and Sapper Hill."

He delivered the information at a deliberate pace so we could make notes, and Dale could keep up with the stick. He continued.

"The info on the cards speaks for themselves, the chalk represents streams, and the string represents roads."

He then described the area in detail, our objective. Just what was on the model, no in depth information as of yet, just what meant what on the model. Also there way small cardboard signs placed on our objective, each named Wing Forward, Fly Half, and Full Back, the Commanding Officer being a big rugby fan.

He then proceeded to go into detail about the "Ground" we would be operating on route to Longdon, and also in depth detail of the mountain itself. Longdon was an imposing feature, 600 feet at its highest point, and dominated the surrounding moorland for quite some distance. The mountain consisted of a series of large rock runs that was steep at the western end and petered off towards Wireless Ridge in the east. The model was formed in such a way; Longdon looked like a headless dinosaur skeleton partially dug up with Wireless Ridge as its tail.

With the ground part of his orders delivered to us he then went into his "Situation" paragraph. He went into detail about the bigger picture with regards to the campaign as it stood at the moment, and what effect our attack on Longdon would have on the enemy in the grand scheme of things. A lot of it, to be honest, I felt was well above my pay scale, but knowledge is power, so they say. He then went into detail about the enemy occupying Longdon, morale, strength, weapons, routine, patrol programme that was virtually nonexistent since the skirmish with our guys a few nights ago, possible future intentions, likely arcs for their heavy machine guns, possible fall back plan, minefields, killing areas, you name it. The Patrols guys had really done their homework, night after night going forward to gather as much information for us as possible so hopefully there were no surprises on the day of the race. In a nutshell, if we hit the enemy hard enough, they will fold, as proven at Goose Green. It was at this stage the whole magnitude of what we were about to embark on was beginning to catch up with me. I could feel my stomach tighten with pre-match nerves that had not been present since we were being soaked through on the landing craft on the way to the beach in broad daylight. Things were suddenly very real; we could well be killing the enemy very shortly, or getting killed by them. I glanced around at some of the other guys, if they were in the same boat as me; they kept a good poker face, and wasn't letting on. Once he finished going into detail about Friendly forces, we were pretty much all seated in front of him with regards to the Company and its attachments for the attack, he also announced that our Second Battalion was in reserve should the opportunity arise to exploit success.

He then gave us our mission statement.

"B Company, your mission is to clear Fly Half and Full Back. Be prepared to support C Company when they attack Wireless Ridge, in order to clear the enemy from within the 3 PARA boundary".

He allowed a pause, and then repeated the mission statement. This is done so you are left in no doubt what you are there to do. Fly Half and Full Back was pretty much the whole feature that is Mount Longdon. Wing Forward was a task for A Company.

He then moved on to his "Execution" paragraph.

"Guys, firstly we will deal with the prelim moves prior to our advance to the Start Line. Straight after these orders, we will move up to the western base of Mount Vernet in assault order. Bergens will be left stacked in Section lines just outside your trenches. We will march in slow time to Mount Vernet, where my Command Group will move into over watch of the objective for any last minute adjustment to my orders."

Justin's Command Group consisted of his radio operator, all the Platoon Commanders and their radio operators, plus the attached group commanders. The aim of this was should he want to fine tune his plan, he could inform the various commanders who would pass what was relevant down to whoever needed to know. What I wasn't looking forward to was the pain in the arse march up the hill across them bastard rock fields, where you are just asking for a busted ankle.

"Once in position, we will wait for the order from the Commanding Officer to begin our approach to this stream junction here."

Dale used the stick to point out the feature on the model.

"Order of March will be 6 Platoon, and then my group, minus Platoon Commanders, then 5 Platoon, Sergeant Major's group, followed up by 4 Platoon."

Dale's group would consist of himself, his Radio Op, our Company clerk, who now assumed the role of ammo donkey and runner, Company medics, and 4 Platoon Commander, who could react on Dale's orders from Justin to deploy his Platoon forward should there be a need for it.

"We will stop short of the stream junction, and we will meet up with a team from Patrols who will guide us into the start line prior to our attack."

Dale traced the route with the stick as Justin dictated. Justin continued.

"Once in position, 4 Platoon left, 5 in the centre, and 6 on the right, advancing on a broad front, you must be aware that we will have A Company to our left, clearing Wing Forward, and Patrols to our right, who will prevent any enemy reinforcements from Tumbledown, and also keep eyes on Wireless Ridge. C Company will be behind us in reserve, ready to move through us onto Wireless Ridge when we have cleared the main feature."

Justin paused for any questions. There were none from anyone; I think everyone had the same dreaded feeling as me now, since I noticed a few of the audience looking rather uneasy. The plan sounded straight forward, I think it's the fact that this is for real, no more training.

He then went onto a series of "Actions On" measures should anything happen that could cock up the whole mission, people getting injured on route, people getting lost, enemy sees us before we get sorted out at the Start Line, etc, etc.

It was at this stage that handed the floor over to Dale, who then delivered the "Service Support" paragraph. This was a Sergeant Major's bag. He went into detail with regards to Casualty procedure, Prisoner handling, what he wanted certain people to carry in their gear and where, Ammo resupply, anything that involved administration for the coming operation, Dale went to town, and I noticed all the Corporals and Sergeants scribbling like mad into their notebooks. He then allowed pens to cool before he then went to town on random people in the form of questioning them on what he had told them. If they got it wrong, he didn't bollock them, he patiently re-issued the information, it was important that everyone, not just commanders knew what he wanted and when it was to be done, it could involve taking or saving lives.

Justin then took over again, thanking Dale for his method of getting the message across. This last part of the orders was "Command and Signals" this was very much the business of whom was to assume command should anyone be taken out of the fight for whatever reason, and what radio frequencies we needed to be on for the operation, etc. He concluded this paragraph with asking the Artillery Observer, who would be in charge of our Artillery support for a time check. The Artillery Captain announced the time in two minutes time, and this prompted all watch wearers, especially Commanders to prepare their own watches for the countdown to the time stated by him. Once done, he then sat back down; Justin was back in the driver's seat.

"In summary guys, we are going to take Longdon and those fuckers sat on it, Stanley is just twelve miles away, and I'm pissed off with being cold, wet and tired longer than I have to be, I'm sure you will agree."

The lads broke into a muffled cheer; he raised a hand to calm it down.

"Guys, make no mistake, by what we've heard about Goose Green, we won't have it all our own way, just trust your commanders, and do your job. If all else fails, make your way to the top of Longdon, understood?"

We all nodded. This was it.

"Right then, get your shit squared, my Command group will take the lead to Vernet in an hour, see you there."

With that, we all began to disperse, amid the hustle and bustle; a few of the lads cast their eye over the model for a few minutes just to get the lay of the land in their heads. Jamie and I quickly made our way back to our position to do some last minute kit adjustments. The cold fog began to lift, and you could now see the whole settlement was a hive of activity. To the east of the settlement, I could see one of the companies, don't know which one, making its way in two columns up the long gradient towards Mount Estancia.

"Kit on, and stack your bergens" shouted Danny, and I went through the same routine of placing my kit on. Quilted suit packed away, webbing on, belts of ammo wrapped around my torso, barrel bag on, and helmet on. A few of the lads were sat once again outside their trenches, smoking, or picking their noses, enjoying the calm before the impending storm. I was getting nervous, make no mistake, but I was comfortable in knowing I wasn't the only one. Jamie looked over to me.

"Things are going to get real tasty soon, my man."

If that was his attempt at comforting me, it wasn't working. He was worried, he must be, and I defy anyone who was not nervous about the coming operation. I knew it was pre-match nerves, but I now started to question what I'd let myself in for. This clearly was a case of me joining the Army for a world of adventure and it was now cashing in on my obligation to the country. Was the way I was feeling what them poor sods felt in the trenches just before going over the top at the Somme? Or them guys just about to jump into Normandy? It must be. The fact is it was my generations turn to fight, plain and simple. Now man up Archie, you fucking dick.

"Prepare to move" was the order called down the line, with that we clambered to our feet. Abit of jumping up and down and shifting of kit to get comfy, usual stuff, I'd given up trying to get boxer shorts out of the crack of my arse, I had too much kit on. We started to move slowly towards the eastern side of the settlement, and we slowly fell into column and began our march up to Mount Vernet. We crossed a small road bridge as we came out of Estancia and the turned left and headed North East uphill towards the many rock fields that surrounded Vernet. The pace was very slow when the lead elements started to pick their way around the worse of the rock fields. I like to think Justin wanted to keep injuries on the way to our objective to a minimum. A few of the rock traverses were abit technical and slippery, but we managed to stay on our feet, as we picked our way slowly towards our concentration area. I was sweating like a lunatic, no change there, but I'd past caring about that. I kept glancing right, hoping to catch a glimpse of Longdon, but Justin's route ensured we were out of sight of the objective; probably something to do with it being covered in enemy was a good bet. After a couple of hours of rock balancing, slipping and sliding, we got into our concentration area on the western side of Vernet. Justin then took all those in his command group further up the feature to get eyes on the objective. We just sat tight, and got comfortable, with the quilted suit display team deploying in record time. I hoped we were not staying here long, I would not want to try and sleep here, bits of rock sticking out of the ground everywhere, and I could see any flat smooth ground anywhere. Accommodation wise, we clearly had it too good at Teal and Estancia, despite the cold.

Jamie got a brew on the go, and I could smell the aroma of cigarettes drifting across our position, it was now a case of sitting tight until the order came to move out towards our RV with our patrol guides. I'm sure it was getting colder, I took my leather gloves off so I could sort out my boot laces, and by the time I had my gloves back on, my hands were in pain. After a little while, my hands returned back their usual state. Apart from drink tea, and pick our noses, putting cam cream on, there wasn't much else to do until the Boss got back from Justin's Command group. There may be slight changes to the plan, but I doubt it. I'm no expert tactician by any stretch of the imagination, but what Justin gave in his orders was straight forward enough for us Private soldiers to understand, but that's the point, if it's all going wrong, every man whatever their rank needs to know what needs to be achieved. In training, we were forever being told to pay attention to the plan; you are only one bullet away from being in charge.

The Boss was now back, and no change to the orders, the plan was set. B Company were the lead Company to the RV with Patrols, this would ensure we would be in the right order of March for Patrols to guide us into our Start Line. We were starting to lose light now, and it wouldn't be long before it got dark. Justin and Dale were doing the rounds, chatting to every single one of us and shaking our hands, and cracking the odd joke. He came over to where me and Jamie were sat, and we clambered to our feet to greet him.

"Alright lads?"

"Yes, Sir" I replied.

"Archie, what's on your mind mate?" Dale asked.

I just shook my head, and let out a low whistle.

"This is the real deal, isn't it?"

"Yep" Justin replied "Pretty much, doesn't mean you have to like it, me neither."

Dale placed his hand on my shoulder.

"You'll be fine, remember, and just make your way to the top."

"No problems Sir."

Dale looked over to Jamie.

"You okay?"

"I'm fine thanks Sir, how are you?" Jamie answered.

"Okay" Dale grinned "okay".

They shook our hands and moved on to the next group of lads sitting amongst the rocks. We sat down and I rummaged through my smock pockets for some chocolate. I broke it open and offered Jamie some; he waved his hand in refusal. Not like him.

"You ok mate?" I asked in a low voice.

"Not really Archie, I'm shitting myself"

Now it was my turn to comfort him.

"So am I, we all are, didn't you see Justin and Dale, this is their first fight too, and we are all in the same boat mate"

He grinned and nodded.

"You're right."

"Mount up" shouted Dale. We struggled to our feet again, got our gear comfortable and shook hands. The light was fading fast, I just wished the bloody shit weather would fade with it, no such luck, in fact, change that; I'll keep the weather in exchange for no Argentinians on our objective. If only. We stood around waiting for 4 Platoon to head off over the rise towards our RV, shortly followed by Justin's group. By the time we moved out it was as good as dark. We were on.

7

The full moon breaking through the dispersing clouds made our picking through the rock fields easier, as we could see where we were placing our feet. The cold night air was no less savage, large vapour clouds marked the positions of almost everyone as we picked our way through, through both our breath and our sweating under our combat loads. Most of us gunners still had our machine guns on our shoulders, as this helped us keep balance as we clambered over the more technical parts of these rivers of rock. As much as we tried, remaining totally silent on our approach was almost impossible; the scraping of boots on jagged rock, the odd clatter of belt ammunition wrapped around a soldier's torso was quite prominent in the night air. Some of my nervousness had faded, since the time for thinking was over, and we were getting on with what we received a salary for. After what felt like an eternity, we started to clear the rock fields and forward left of our column as we descended off the high ground was a large cluster of reflective surfaces. As we slowly passed on their right side, it became clear to me that they were ponds of standing water, nothing more. We then began to veer left and hand rail a small trickling stream on our right side, with the ponds on our left. The soggy ground began to suck at our boots, with the odd rock to trip you up thrown in for good measure. We continued to follow the stream for some time until the column ground to a halt. Up ahead I noticed people beginning to kneel down taking up alternate arcs, facing left and right of our column. I got to face right, not that there was very much to look at. On the other side of the stream the ground climbed gradually and was what appeared to be flat at the top, not much else. I looked left and could see a figure moving slowly down the line. As the figure drew close, I could make out John's profile.

"We are just short of the RV" he whispered, "Patrols will then guide us to our start line, okay?"

Those who could hear him nodded, including me, and with that he moved back to his place in the line. Unlike our other marches across the island, there was no aroma of cigarettes or hexamine blocks, it was full on tactical, talking and noise to a minimum. It wasn't long before the column began to get to its feet and start shuffling forward again. I'd changed from having the gimpy across a shoulder to now slung across my front ready for action, we were right on the enemy's doorstep now. We slowly made our way forward, the stream now started to get wider and noisier with more water trickling through it. With the full moon and clear sky, the surrounding moorland was very well lit and the shadows cast by random outcrops of rock made the whole venture even creepier. We eventually arrived at what appeared to be a busy stream junction. Patrols Company was here in force both providing protection for the RV, plus also picking up their respective companies to guide to their start lines. As we made our way closer, I could make out soldiers stood in the stream. Fuck that, talk about making your bollocks shrink. Our progress was almost at a snail pace now, and it wasn't long before I could see why, the guys in the water, which turned out to be Royal Engineers attached to us, had laid on a series of ladders and planks of wood to get us across the stream with our heavy loads. God bless 'em stood in the stream making sure we stayed dry, nice one lads. When it came to my turn, I had to traverse a ladder, and the Engineers each side of me basically grabbed my arms without ceremony and whispered instructions to me as I placed my feet on the ladder rungs, almost like a parent talking a toddler through their first steps. As I got to the other side they let go and gave me the thumbs up, done. We may have been the combat troops, but this was sure as shit their crossing site, and you danced to their tune, they didn't care what rank you was, or your status in the unit, you all got the same treatment, and rightly so. We slowly filed on making room for the other lads crossing, and then stopped to take a knee, to allow for the remainder of the company to cross.

Sometime later, after freezing our tits off waiting for the company to complete the crossing, I noticed Dale make his way up the line to the front of the column; this clearly meant the company was now complete again, since the Company Sergeant Major would normally be at the back of the line. Before long we got to our feet and began to move forward again, and as we shuffled on, we passed Dale, who was counting us through, one of his many duties in battle, making sure we hadn't lost anyone, through injury or just plain lost. We started to move right, away from the stream bank but hugging into the gradient on our right, so not to expose us to Longdon as much as possible. We continued on this course for some time until our cover on the right began to reduce until there was nothing but open ground and there was Mount Longdon to our forward right, huge, looming, and to be honest, very intimidating. The model didn't lie; it did look like dinosaur remains, huge sheets of rock sticking out of the mountain like a huge ribcage. That dreaded feeling had now returned, to me it felt like every Argentine soldier on that mountain was just sat there looking at our column, waiting for the right time to ambush us. Our column moved around to the right and began to slowly make its way up the valley that took us directly in front of the mountain. With every couple of steps I kept peering left, because I felt so exposed in our current position, surely their sentries must have seen us by now. Please be asleep. I was hoping they had got up and fucked off back into Stanley for a pint, anything that would have this night pass without incident. After a short period of time, we began to pass soldiers kneeling and laying down to our left facing Longdon. 4 Platoon were now at their Start Line, it was our turn next. The Patrols guys had actually placed white strips of tape down to mark where every sub unit was going to form up, this clearly said to me that these guys had already been here, taking their chances with the enemy sentries, truly remarkable, these guys were without doubt experts in their craft.

We began to get placed into our respective positions, this part of the operation remained in the hands of Patrols Company, they had Private soldiers, who were to be fair above average intelligence, switched on operators placing companies of men into position for the up and coming battle, a task not to be taken lightly. In front of me in the line was Zane, he was basically being put exactly where the Patrols guy wanted him to lay, no ifs or buts. Then it was mine and Jamie's turn, since we worked as a pair, a gun team, me as the gunner and Jamie helping me manage the gun and also feed the thing. This Patrols guy walked over to me and took me gently by the arm and led me to the spot where he wanted me, I then un slung the gun, slowly deployed its bipod legs to avoid them springing open with a clatter, and lay down in the grass that was just about long enough to cover my barrel muzzle. Our guide then lay down to my right, almost on top of me and gave me a thumbs down gesture, which was the NATO sign for enemy and then in a karate chop motion pointed his arm in the direction of Longdon. There be enemy. I nodded, with that he gave me a gentle dig in the shoulder and then got up and placed Jamie next to me, carrying out the same ritual for his benefit. He then got to his feet, and then went to fetch the next guy. I looked at Jamie, who just pulled a face and winked at me. Forever the comedian.

The moon made Longdon very prominent in the darkness, from our position the right side of the mountain looked like a large saddle feature with huge rock faces at each end, and to its left was a series of jagged rock runs that looked all the more sinister with huge shadows cast by the moon. I looked left and right of our Start Line, small columns of breath vapour marked where the guys had been placed. The wind picked up slightly making my shivering all the more intense. I could hear a series of clicks to my left. As it grew louder, it very quickly dawned on me what it was, and my stomach turned over. Bayonets were being fitted. I tried my hardest to not vomit, but I managed to keep it in my mouth and force it down again, burning my throat. This shit wasn't funny anymore, I looked at Jamie waiting for him to fit his, but he slowly shook his head. Maybe he felt fighting as a gun team would only be made more difficult if a bayonet was being swung around whilst helping me. I looked into the left and saw people getting to their feet and starting to move forward. I clambered to my feet and tried to remain calm as I stowed the bipod legs. I looked left and right, the whole company was on its feet moving forward, and the ground rose gently and care had to be taken not to trip on rocks hidden in the ankle deep frozen grass that crunched under our feet. Progress was slow and steady; Longdon loomed over head, but didn't appear to get any closer. The gradient began to rise more prominently now, making me breath heavier, we were just short of the first series of large rocks that rose above us.

Then there was a loud thud to our rear left, followed by a loud scream. I could hear people calling "man down", and "medic". 4 Platoon? I didn't know. We all went to ground; I was on my belly in record time with Jamie crawling in next to me, but this time on my left. We scanned the ground ahead, there was a lot of commotion coming from 4 platoon by the sounds of things, not good. I started to hear chatter and shouting to my front, I couldn't make out what it was, but it quickly dawned on me that it wasn't us. There was a pop, a whoosh and a plume of smoke from a cluster of rocks above us and another pop above as our entire position was lit up by a flare. The shouting in the rocks above us got all the more excitable, they see us, they can fucking see us!

Green and orange tracer began to stream down to our left since it was 4 Platoon that was making a lot of noise initially, but their fire then shifted to us. Rounds were thumping into the ground around our position and sparks flew as they smashed into rock hidden in the grass. I could see a series of muzzle flashes from amongst the rock above us, so I cocked the gun and began to fire short bursts at the muzzle flashes. All this seemed to do was attract their attention, and green and orange tracer then smashed and thudded all around us, fuck!

"Move forward, move forward, get to some cover" someone shouted.

No one moved, the flares had us caught like rabbits in headlights.

"Fucking move" Danny shouted.

We got up mob handed, and dashed forward, grabbing the gun by the carrying handle, I legged it to the first cluster of rocks I could hide behind. Just as the light faded from one flare, another took its place, we were so caught in the open, and we had to get in amongst the rocks. Jamie was right on my tail as we slid in behind some decent cover. I tried to site the gun in a decent position with the legs down, but I was too exposed, as tracer smashed into our cover. Legs up, lower profile. As I tried to get into position, our rocks would get hit with incoming fire. Jamie would lean out to his left and snap off a few shots with his SLR, but would then duck back in just as rounds would smash into our cover again. Pinned down here. As another flare lit up our position, I could see all order of formation had gone out of the window, the guys were literally behind cover in various sized groups just trying to get the upper hand. We had a fair idea which muzzle flash above us was giving us trouble, and some of the lads were giving it back as I could see red tracer splashing all over that position, and for a little while that position would be silent, but would start up again, maybe with a new gunner.

The din around us was tremendous, machine gun fire, screaming, shouting, you name it. I took the barrel bag off as the strap was really chaffing my neck. Jamie then grabbed my arm and pointed to the left. I could make out John shouting at me, but amongst the noise, I couldn't make out what he wanted. It became apparent, when everyone dashed out of cover and took a bound forward, I quickly grabbed the gun as Jamie already began sprinting forward. As I legged it after him, I noticed him jump over a small group of rocks, as I got close, green and orange tracer began to thud and smash into the ground just right of me, I changed direction and went for the rocks Jamie hurdled. I then tripped, and got a face full of timber and peat as I fell through the floor onto a soft and squirming surface. I was winded as I landed on the gun, my face killing me after getting a face full of mountain. I rolled over and propped myself against a peat wall of sorts. The soft squirming floor then started shouting

Spanish at me and as I scrambled for my weapon it became more animated. A drifting flare above lit up what appeared to be a face, I fired, this face shattered like an egg, showering the bunker and me in brain, skull, teeth and blood. The gunfire rendered me deaf as my ears rang. Out of the darkness another face and a pair of hands appeared and lunged at me, grabbing my throat and face. I grabbed at the wrists and attempted to prize them away.

"Jamie, Jamie" I screamed, muffled because my ears were still ringing.

This guys was screaming also, didn't have a clue what he wanted, probably help the same as me.

"Jamie, Jamie, help me"

I managed to get my right boot into his stomach area and push, whilst using my gloved hands to squeeze his wrists as hard as I could which loosened his grasp, and I managed to overpower him and pin him to the floor. Still in control of his hands, I head butted him, again, and again.

"You fuck, you fucker, fuck you" I spat in his face.

He was still screaming out for help.

I smashed my head into his face again, and again, and again.

"You fucker, fuck you, you fucking fuck" I roared.

I continued to plough my head into his bare face until he was silent.

I let go of his wrists, and his arms flopped to the floor. I scrambled back against the wall. Soaked with sweat, I caught my breath, and in the drifting light of the flares searched for my weapon.

I saw in the fading light, the gimpy underneath the legs of my sparring partner. I crawled over and grabbed his right leg and swung it other his left. I pulled at the weapon but it was still caught under his body weight. I then grabbed the right side of his duvet jacket and gave an almighty heave and rolled him onto his front, freeing up the gun. I grabbed it with both hands and scrambled back to my end of the trench. I clutched the gun tightly in my arms and rested my head against the trench wall. The ringing in my ears began to fade and the violent din outside returned in full force. I could hear rounds snapping overhead, rounds smashing off rock, thudding into peat. Men screaming, swearing and crying. I had to rejoin my Platoon, as I leant forward to get to my feet, pain exploded through my head as something hot and solid punched into the left side of my face, pinning me to the trench wall, and a bright red glow blinded me.

"Who the fuck are you?" growled a voice, clearly English.

"Archie, Archie" I panicked, "5 Platoon"

The solid object was released from the side of my face and the red glow disappeared instantly, all my night vision ruined, as the trench was now full of red drifting blobs as I tried to focus again in the dark.

"You've made a right mess of these guys" said the voice again, "can you walk?"

I nodded, and with that a hand grabbed hold of my webbing strap and yanked me out of the trench, I clutched the gun even tighter, so not to drop it. I was pulled out of the trench and forced onto my back; my helper placed a knee gently on my chest and began talking.

"Yeah, roger that, I've got one of yours here, show red light, make yourself known to me."

As I regained focus, my helper was none other than Dale. He must have heard me and came to investigate. Chaos reigned all around us, and he was knelt up, pinning me underneath him, trying to get me back to my Platoon.

"Show red light, over."

A few seconds passed.

"Yep, seen, I'm coming to you, sit tight."

He looked back down to me.

"You okay?"

"Yes Sir"

"Good, sort your weapon out, I'm taking you to meet up with 5 again, understand?"

He released me and I rolled onto my front and made sure the gun was still in working order, belt untwisted, barrel still on, done.

"Ready" I called out above the gunfire.

"Okay, let's go"

He pulled me to my feet pushing me past the trench, as I peered back he threw a grenade into the trench and ran past me. There was a loud thud and a huge plume of white phosphorous smoke billowed out of the hole. I picked up the pace and caught up with Dale as he sought refuge behind rocks with some other guys. We looked back, as green and orange tracer splashed all over the burning trench. The enemy above wasn't taking any chances and hosing anything that moved below them. A hand grabbed my shoulder, in the drifting light of flares, I could make out Zane talking to Dale, and we were back with 5 Platoon. Dale then turned to me.

"Here you go Archie boy, no more hero stuff okay?"

I nodded, and then Zane pulled me over to him, and shouted into my ear.

"Right then, we've cleared some of the bunkers, but this fucker up front is holding the company up."

He peered around our cover and pointed at the offending machine gun post, I leant out behind him so I could see where it was. We leant back in.

"He's chewed up the platoon pretty bad, Danny, John, and a couple of the guys are forward now trying to knock him out. 6 Platoon are trying to come around on the right side, but they have problems of their own. 4 Platoon are trying to get into the rock runs to our left. These bastards have got their shit sited proper, know what I mean?"

I nodded; I think he was trying to tell me we were not having it all our own way. The problem position was just below the skyline of the saddle, and until we dealt with it, we were not going anywhere. Then there was a series of grenades thudding all over the problem position. We leant out of cover to observe, the position was smouldering and there were a couple of our guys milling about in front of it. As a flare burst overhead, the whole mountainside was drowned in a brilliant white light, the two guys in front of the knocked out bunker were instantly splashed in green tracer, one of whom burst into a cloud of white phosphorous smoke, the incoming fire must of hit his grenades, the other hit with numerous rounds that took his face off and bits of his torso flew off. His body ending up in a sitting position against the front of the bunker. The horror show ended as the flare light faded out. Zane looked at me.

"I hope they weren't our guys"

Another flare burst into life above us, and we looked at the body sat in front of the bunker. As the flare drifted, and the shadows moved, it looked like the body was moving, and then another burst of green and orange splashed all over it, more pieces flicked off, but the body stayed sat up. The fucker still firing at it, was forward right of us and as the flare light faded out, I could make out some of our guys scrambling around to the right to deal with it. In the darkness, there was a loud thud as a grenade went in to the bunker, followed by a series of screams from inside which lasted what seemed like ages. Two rifle shots brought the screaming to a close. Position taken. Slowly and quite rightly cautiously, we broke cover and made our way up towards the saddle. As we drew close to where the two guys were shot up, it was clearly evident they were our guys. We made a wide berth around the smouldering figure in case anymore of his ammo cooked off in the heat, but the guy sat in front of the smouldering bunker was plain to see. Jaw shot away, helmet caved in on one side, his left arm almost severed. As we picked our way passed the bunker itself, you couldn't help noticed the aroma of human shit coming from it. Did the occupants defecate in the bunker? Or did their bowels get ripped open when they were smashed with grenades? Who knows? Who cares? Position clear.

8

Word comes round to sit tight before we committed ourselves over the saddle. The enemy were full of surprises tonight, and their concealment of bunkers was excellent. They wouldn't open fire until you was right on top of them which made for very grim fighting. More of our guys were making their way up behind us. These guys were gun and MILAN teams, stopping short with us before we went over the top. I looked over to the right side of the saddle and saw in the low light a figure make his way through the rocks towards me, jingling and rattling as he walked. As he pulled up next to us I noticed it was Jamie. He was draped in shitloads of belt ammo.

"Hello stranger", he called out, as he stripped off his load, "where have you been?"

I didn't want to talk about the bunker I fell in.

"Got caught up on some wire, Dale helped me get loose."

"Man," Jamie shook his head, "this is some crazy shit"

I nodded. We tucked into some rocks as more flares burst over head, as the flare drifted across the mountain, it was clearly evident what the company had been through up to this point. There were a series of smouldering bunkers. Bodies, both theirs and ours were left as they fell, some in grotesque positions. Nothing like what Hollywood would have you believe. Our part of the mountain was relatively quiet, 4 and 6 Platoon however, were having a right time of it, grenades thudding in bunkers, people shouting and screaming, rounds pinging and smashing off rocks, quite a soundtrack.

"Listen up" it was Davo.

"4 Platoon are getting chewed up bad trying to get into the rock runs. My Section is going to back track the way we came and reinforce their push up the mountain. The remainder of the Platoon are going to push over the saddle shortly and provide close protection for these gun and MILAN teams, everyone clear?"

Where was John? Danny? Boss?

There were muffled replies and nodding heads.

"Right then" Davo continued "my Section grab your shit, let's go."

We made our way back down the way we had come to the base of the saddle, using the flare light to our advantage, allowing our progress through the rocks and burning bunkers easier. Once we almost got to the base of the feature we then skirted around to the right which would lead us to 4 Platoon at the base of the rock runs. We stopped short, Davo getting on the radio to let 4 Platoon know we were coming. I didn't fancy getting shot up by my own side. We took cover in a cluster of rocks and waited. In the flare light, I took a look at who was still with us. Davo, me, Jamie, Zane, Leighton. Shit, was that it? They can't be all dead surely? I was not looking forward to joining 4 Platoon. Just on the other side of a huge slab of rock that separated us, 4 Platoon were in a full on brawl with an enemy that was not having any of it.

Davo got to his feet.

"Let's go guys"

We scrambled after him and we slowly made our way around the large rock, and we were greeted by what looked like a pile of logs. Next to the logs was a figure kneeling down with a radio on his back. The soldier was talking into a handset.

"What do you mean, anti tank gun?"

Davo tried to get his attention, to no avail.

"Who? They have? where? I need more information than that, have they got an anti tank gun or not?"

He looked around and got the fright of his life. Us bunch of menacing goons peering at him through the darkness. He held his hand up to us, and spoke back into the handset.

"Right, get off the skyline, and stay alert for those fuckers still alive above you, got it? Out."

He then turned to us.

"Alright lads, please tell me your platoon is making better progress than us. We are getting the shit kicked out of us. We've got two alleyways of rock to clear, and they are dug in tight, these fuckers aren't giving up ground for shit, let me show you."

He led us further around the rock to a point where we could see what he meant by alleyways. Huge slabs of rock that could almost pass for prison walls, they were that high, with the enemy perched all over them firing down at 4 Platoon. The alley was made hard going also by the fact that it was uphill. This part of the objective looked like a bastard to clear out. We then went back to our previous position by the pile of logs. A flare burst above us and revealed the pile of logs for what it actually was; these logs were wearing camouflage clothing. 4 Platoon dead. I turned away trying to force down the vomit that was flooding my mouth, too late. I stepped away from the group and sprayed the grass and my boots with the contents of my stomach. The burning throughout my core was intense; I felt a hand on my shoulder as I tried to calm down my retching.

"You ok matey?"

I looked up and Davo was grinning at me, and gave me a friendly wink.

"Yeah, sorry, not what they show you in the brochure."

The bodies were covered in a poncho, which covered the grimness of their demise. Just seeing their legs and boots stacked up like firewood, which was just too much for me, reminded me of old pictures of Stalingrad or Auschwitz you see in the history books. I caught the gaze of their Platoon Sergeant.

"I couldn't leave em in the open" he stated "getting shredded over and over again by grenades and incoming. My reserve Section played undertaker for a while, not nice, not nice at all. The Boss will be down in a minute, he's at the top of the alley nearest the summit, he will be glad to see his new reserve Section, thanks for volunteering."

And the hits just keep on coming.

While we waited for 4 Platoons Boss to come down, we listened to the carnage unfolding above us. The gun and MILAN teams were now committed and you could hear a horrendous amount of firepower going down range. There were huge explosions rocking the backside of Longdon. Not too sure who was dishing it out, but it was intense. I hoped the guys up on the saddle were ok, we'd taken a mauling getting up there, I just hoped they could hold it. The flares above us continued to fade out and instantly be replaced by fresh ones. As they drifted across the mountain, they revealed our grim surroundings. The pile of 4 Platoon dead, bloody bandages, empty ammo containers, brass cases from heavy gunfights, all the debris you expect from such a fight. We could see in the flare light people coming down the alley, a couple keeping their eyes peeled at the top of the rocks, the others carrying wounded personnel. As they got close to us, we could see that 4 Platoon were also badly mauled by tonight's efforts. Our host called them over and they went about putting the wounded behind cover, a little distance from their dead friends. Medics who had been with them in the assault up the alley looked in no better shape, but went about their duties, getting the guys patched up as best they could.

One of the soldiers walked over to us, and outstretched his hand.

"Thanks for coming down to help us out, I'm Jay, O.C, 4 Platoon"

Davo accepted the hand.

"Hello Sir, crazy shit we are in yes?"

He nodded.

"I've got a Section holding the top of the alley, but at this time not committed on the top. They've got some heavy shit up there keeping us pinned in. Up on the cliff to our right, someone is rolling grenades in, hence our current condition. 5 Platoon are slowly dealing with them, and trying to protect the gun teams at the same time, as they are very exposed. They've got some kind of flak gun up there, and some kind of anti-tank weapon. Our Artillery is trying to knock them out as we speak. Christ knows what's happened to this naval gunfire we are meant to have."

We just looked at each other.

"Justin and Dale are with 6 Platoon, trying to get them forward, but we've walked straight into the lion's den here, a very strong defensive screen."

No shit, the dead and wounded were rising in number.

"We need to get back up there, and deal with them fuckers up on the cliff, all set?"

We were ready to go, let's get this thing done. Jay set off at a patrol pace, followed by us in single file. We kept to the left side of the alley as we began to climb. One couldn't help but to keep peering up at the right side, looking for potential targets. We got about halfway up, when some rocks up to the right gave way, all of us swung our barrel muzzles up there instinctively. The rocks clattered down the wall, and one of them exploded.

There was an almighty thud, and the right side of my face stung like someone had given it a right proper slap. My ears exploded into a high pitch ring. I fell onto my hands and knees and as I looked up I could see Jay and Davo firing like mad up at the cliff. The ringing in my head drowned out any soundtrack of battle. They dived to the floor, and I copied them as the ground vibrated with another big thud. I stayed put with my face planted in the peat as I felt the ground thud underneath me a few more times. We are all going to die. I felt a hand roughly grab my right shoulder and flip me over. Above me, was Davo who would then knock me across the same side of the face that still stung like a bastard. Slowly the soundtrack of combat returned to me in full force.

"You okay?" Davo called out, "can you walk?"

I couldn't feel anything wrong with me, apart from being broadsided with the ultimate hangover.

"Yeah, did we get em?"

"I'm not sure" Davo replied," 5 Platoon are going to have to clear em out before we try and push up again."

Davo and Jamie pulled me to my feet and we made our way back down to the Platoon RV at the bottom of the alley. As we made our way, Jamie piped up.

"You're not having much luck tonight are you?" He wasn't wrong, but I'd rather be abit battered than dead, wrapped in a poncho. Jamie led me to where the 4 Platoon wounded were sat. Straight away, one of their medics tended to me, with a red torch light, he examined the side of my face.

"I don't think you've got anything to worry about mate" he stated," I think you just got pebble dashed, I would give you pain relief, but I think I'm going to need it later."

Fair cop. Relief washed through me, by the sounds of things, the grenade did nothing more than ring my bell for me. I fished out one of my water bottles, and took several greedy gulps. Despite the intense cold of the night air, the cold water was refreshing. I took time to take in my surroundings. Off to my left down near our Start Line, I could just make out a load of dark shapes slowly making their way towards us. I stood up and gingerly made my way to where those still fit to fight had gathered.

"Look out there, can you see em?" I pointed in the direction of the slow moving shapes.

"A Company" Jay announced. "They were meant to clear the open spur to our North, but they've been getting alot of harassing fire from Snipers and mortars, by what is being said over the radio."

A Company by the looks of things was attempting to seek refuge behind the mountain, since their objective appeared to be untenable to remain on for a long period of time. Up above us we heard the thud of grenades at the top of the problem cliff, followed by some God awful screaming which continued for some time. We looked at Jay.

"5 are taking care of things for us, get ready to move."

Fresh screams could now be heard, but no grenades. At one point, there was someone up there begging to be spared, and then another scream that went right through you. The scream then became a muffled gargle which after a while faded into silence. The grim purpose of the bayonet was being employed by 5 Platoon. I shuddered at the thought of such business. 5 Platoon had taken a mauling getting up to the summit, and their good manners guide had long since been ditched in a burning bunker or two. There comes a point in a battle when you just need to get the grim and unthinkable done, such is the job description for a soldier.

Jay began to lead us back up the alley, once again keeping our eyes peeled high right as we climbed to join the remainder of 4 Platoon at the top. As we got near the top I could see red, orange and green tracer streaming past from right to left, which didn't make any sense. After thinking it over, it made perfect sense, our gun teams must be using enemy ammunition, and after all, they did have the same weapon systems as us, give or take some minor alterations. The gun teams were dishing it out in spades to whoever was on the eastern end of Longdon. MILAN missiles went roaring down range to their targets. The din was incredible. All of a sudden there was a streak of white light from the back end of Longdon and an almighty boom off to our right, our fire support base rendered silent. What the hell was that? We heard a muffled voice on Jay's radio handset.

"Yeah roger that, what's the damage?" He asked. Another muffled response.

"Roger, let me know if there is anything we can do, friendlies will be passing through us soon, out"

We all looked at him for an update. He turned to address us.

"The anti-tank gun we've been trying to knock out has just destroyed a MILAN team complete."

One of the lads gave out a low whistle.

"The fire base is in bad shape, the O.C is just behind 5 Platoon now, with his Artillery observer trying to deal with it, A Company will be passing through us shortly to deal with the main defensive position, and we will become fire support. When we get the word we are going to crawl out of this fucking alley, and we will start engaging the positions as we spot them, understood?"

We nodded. I looked back down the alley and a large group of what could only be A Company was gathering.

9

All sense of time had been lost as far as I was concerned. We'd been in action for several hours now. In that space of time we, as a company had been badly mauled by the looks of things. Back at Estancia, we were probably abit too cock sure about the quality of the Argentine Soldier. So far, what I had experienced and witnessed, these guys were no push over by any stretch of the imagination. Varying in quality, let it be said, but none of them made it easy for us. Our mission as a company was to capture the main feature, but we had just about cleared the Western side of the mountain. Now A Company, though not as planned, were about to push through our positions and finish the job. B Company should not feel inferior about this, we soaked up a lot of punishment, and the guys wrapped in a poncho at the bottom of the rock runs were testament to this, never mind the wounded.

Sat at the top of the alleys we watched some of A Company move up just short of us and Jay made his way down to them. The gun teams on the summit spluttered back into action after getting royally pasted by the anti-tank gun. Red, orange and green tracer streamed across the back end of Longdon at enemies hidden in the darkness, give it to em guys, and fuck them up. Jay moved back up to us.

"Right then, scores on the doors."

He had our attention.

"In a minute we are going to push forward out of here and get eyes on their main position. By what the A Company lads have said, it's in a bowl of sorts, which drops down and away to the North. 1 Platoon are going to join us as a fire base, and 2 Platoon is going to push around the left side of the alleys and start to clear them out. 3 Platoon will be in reserve at the bottom of this alley."

He paused as a series of loud explosions rocked the back end of the mountain, with abit of luck, that fucking anti-tank gun has been dealt with now. Once the bombardment eased off, he continued.

"5 and 6 are going to start pushing forward level with the bowl, to draw fire away from the static and exposed gun teams. Once the main position has been secured, we as a company will move back the way we came to an RAP being set up as we speak near the bottom of the rock runs, okay?"

We all nodded. The Regimental Aid Post, which is run by the Regimental Sergeant Major, is a location for dead and wounded to be collected, from both sides, and a prisoner holding area. Jay moved up to the top of the alley and began to move in a crouch to avoid being seen to a position where we could set up to support A Company. He moved about for some time, probably checking out alternative positions, should we be the focus of the enemy's fury. He then scampered back to us.

"Lets go, keep low"

We set off after him, going firm only when the flares burst above us. Noise was not the issue, just being seen. The noise around us remained horrendous. As the flares faded out we scampered forward towards the jagged teeth like rocks that marked the top of the bowl. Jay sited us one at a time, pointing out likely enemy bunkers. The enemy had proven they were not in the habit of showing their cards too soon. These fuckers remained silent for now. Jamie crawled in besides me, rattling like mad, since he was still draped in hundreds of rounds of belt ammo for me to use. After the initial contact when the battle started were we back together, such is the craziness of these situations. He winked at me.

"Lets give it to these fuckers Archie boy, you shoot, and I feed."

We clashed helmets together; we were on the same page for this one. Just rear left of us, 1 Platoon were on their hands and knees scampering into position. As another flare burst above the far end of the bowl, little could be seen in the shadows of the rocks in the bowl that gave away any sign of enemy, clever bastards. The flare drifted north and as it started to fade, the lead Sections of 2 Platoon were moving into the bowl down to our left. As it went dark the lead Section was smashed by numerous streams of orange and green from all around the bowl. I aimed at the muzzle flash just right of my arc and began firing bursts into it. My own muzzle flash blinded me, but I could still see the where my target was firing from. Burst after burst went into it, but this fucker kept firing.

"Come down slightly" Jamie screamed in my ear, correcting my fire. I did as he said, and began to get somewhere. I hammered my target with some heavy bursts and it would fall silent, for the time being.

"Next target left" Jamie screamed. I switched to the next muzzle flash. Putting heavy bursts into it, but then the original position would burst into life again. I had to remain on the bunker I was committed to and kept firing. Then there was the heart stopping clunk. Stoppage. Shit, shit, shit.

"Stoppage" I cried out, as I grabbed the carry handle and dragged myself and the gun into cover. Staying in the same position to clear a stoppage is something that would seriously upset lovers and mothers, since machine gunners in these situations are pure bullet magnets. The reduced firepower was evident in our group as the enemy were not only dealing with 2 Platoon down below, but also smashing fuck out of the rocks our group was behind. Be quick Archie boy, be real quick. Cock gun, belt off, check for the problem, solve the problem, clear the gun, belt back on, back in action, done. As I got the gun back into the fight, 2 Platoon was fighting for its life in the bowl. They were trying to clear out the bunkers around the base of the bowl anti clockwise. Several guys rushed up just short of a bunker only to be mowed down by another bunker opposite it. As the orange and green splashed into and around them, the lead guy dropped like liquid, bayonet sticking in the ground, which kept him propped up in a kneeling position, the second guy tripped over him and as he scrambled to his feet, was blown in half by rounds hitting the grenades in his pouches, showering him across the front of the position they were trying to assault. The third guy went for the target bunker, but the enemy gunner took his head off with a savage burst from his machine gun. 2 Platoons fury intensified as they gave this particular bunker everything they had, which in turn riddled the propped up body with ricochets and grenade splinters. The gun fell silent, and its occupants had better be dead, I don't think 2 Platoon were in the mood for a quite chat.

We continued to hammer the remaining muzzle flashes, and little by little, A Company started to make progress. Our group and 1 Platoon would smash fuck out of a position, with what was left of 2 Platoon creeping up and throwing grenades in. As the dull thud could be heard we would switch our attention to the next bunker as they went in and made sure them fuckers were finished. Grim but effective. What seemed like forever we slowly dealt with the enemy in the bowl. The bowl was now a mixed bag of random shots and the odd thud of grenades in bunkers. What a night. One of the guys from 1 Platoon crawled over to our group and thanked us for our help, A Company was going to reorganise, and start to push east clearing the remainder of Longdon. We crawled back to the top of the alley. The gun teams on the summit were still taking on targets further east, but not as intense as before the assault into the bowl. Jay rounded us up.

"Good work guys, good shooting."

We didn't feel too pleased about ourselves to be honest, 2 Platoon got chewed up pretty bad in the bowl, but the position was taken. It could of been a lot worse I suppose.

"Once A Company has sorted themselves out, we will make our way to the RAP for a breather, we've earned it. Besides we've got some messed up guys that need taking down there."

He was right, we were in bad shape and on the horizon, daylight was starting to make an appearance. A fog was starting to take hold also, which made the cold even more intense. As my adrenaline began to subside, I began to shiver big time. Partially due to the cold, but also from what had taken place during the course of the night. Hopefully daylight would bring some comfort, and we could sort ourselves out properly in the RAP. We left 1 Platoon on the edge of the bowl, and we slowly made our way back down the alley to 4 Platoon's RV. Upon arrival, we noticed some of the less seriously wounded helping the medics get the real messed up guys sorted. Their Platoon Sergeant rallied up the guys and got us all involved in getting his boys to the RAP which was but a short distance away. One of the guys that needed help was a lad who took a load of grenade fragments to the face. His face was covered in a field dressing, his jaw was exposed and splattered in his blood, and the field dressing had clearly been on a while also, since blood was starting to seep through. I leant down and took him by the arm, which made him jump.

"Hello mate" I began "I'm Archie."

"Hello Archie", he replied, "have you got a cigarette please?"

Bloody typical. I didn't smoke, but I didn't want to disappoint him.

"Hang on, back in a tick." With that I approached one of the other guys for a cigarette. One of the 4 Platoon lads accompanied me back to my patient, lit a cigarette, and put it between his lips.

"There you go Kev, blind or not, get your own fags out in future you tight bastard."

Gallows humour, never fails.

Kev appeared rather content now he had a cigarette on the go, and must have sensed me stood there, as he put his hand out towards me. I grabbed him by the wrist and hauled him to his feet. I steadied him and I then turned around, ensuring his hand had hold of my webbing yoke straps, since I would need my hands free to use the gun if need be. Jay made sure we were all set to go, and slowly led off down out of the alley and began to skirt around to the right. As we cleared an outcrop of craggy rock on our right hand side, I could make out in the early morning mist, a number of figures milling about 200 metres ahead on the right. As we got closer, we could see people helping others into the rocky outcrop. As we drew near, it became apparent this was A Company, bringing their wounded into the RAP from the bowl. A lone figure stood out from the others in the open ground, and judging by his body language, appeared to be running things. Jay turned to us and told us to sit tight, so he could find out where the RSM wanted us. So that was the lone figure. O.B was as old school as they came. I bumped into him a few times, not always on the best of terms, but he was firm but fair, and as he came over to us, the sight before him must have appeared rather pathetic. Stood before him was the shattered remains of 4 Platoon, plus a few from 5. He pointed to an area not too far from the A Company lads.

"Get yourselves in there lads, get yourselves sorted, get a brew and some food in, and keep warm."

He wasn't a brash Sergeant Major on the Drill Square; he was gentle, kind, almost fatherly. We made our way over to where he wanted us, and we set about getting the wounded comfortable. I carefully sat Kev down and helped him out of his fighting gear. I then opened his canvas roll on his belt kit and helped him into his quilted suit, then his waterproofs, just to keep the wind off him. It quickly dawned on me that I had none of my warm kit with me. It was all in my barrel bag where I'd left it during the initial contact. Dickhead. I took my webbing off and sat on it. The cold started to seep in, and I shivered like mad, really wanted my warm kit, I was cold during the night, but during the fighting, you forgot about the cold, since there were more pressing issues at hand. Jamie moved over to me and plonked himself down. He opened his canvas roll, and gave me his waterproof jacket.

"It's not exactly quilted, but it will keep the wind off."

I accepted it and wasted no time getting it on, material rustling and Velcro tearing as I fought my way into it. I must get that barrel bag; it had all my warm kit in it, including my waterproofs. I felt like such an amateur. I should have known better. Jamie winked at me and gave me a cheeky grin. Bastard. I returned his kind gesture by getting the kettle on, rummaging through my pouches for Hot Chocolate and whatever treats I had left from my rations. It wasn't long before we had the biggest mug of Hot Chocolate ever getting dished out between us and the 4 Platoon guys, a couple of sips made you feel like a new man, everything felt good for a while. Once it was finished someone else would get a hot cup of something on the go. Even in battle, there was always time for a cuppa.

Our mood was subdued instantly when we heard the thump of grenades and the cracking of gunfire off to our right along the mountain. A Company was once again clearing out the enemy that still occupied the eastern end of Longdon. Screams were the soundtrack of close combat and the use of bayonets, which went right through you. Please get it done quickly guys, get it done. Jamie nudged my arm and point off to the left. Out of the closing fog, scarecrows of men began to emerge, carrying their grim cargos of wounded men. 5 and 6 Platoon made their way into the RAP. The RSM went to meet them and pointed in our direction. They slowly made their way amongst us, putting the wounded down wherever there was room. Davo stood up and signalled to us with a small hand gesture to move back to 5 Platoon, our secondment to 4 was at an end. We got settled back with our own Platoon. It was comforting to be with more familiar faces. They did however look hollow, shattered shells of men, which was fair enough considering the night we'd just had. Did we look like this to them? They didn't say. Medics clucked around the guys that needed them and out to the front of our location was Justin and Dale. Dale armed with a notebook and pen; I could tell he was in deep consultation with the O.C about company business. It was hardly surprising, B Company had been badly mauled during the night, and not everyone was accounted for. All the wounded, by the looks of things had been brought to the RAP, so that just left the dead. B Company dead. You didn't need to be an atomic scientist to hazard a wild guess what was to be asked of us next. Dale and Justin walked over to address their battered and bloodied Company. Dale did the talking.

"Guys, firstly myself and the O.C would like to thank you tremendously for your efforts during the night, we secured the western end of the objective, but due to heavy resistance, we had to hand the task over to A Company."

He paused to allow it to sink in.

"Having checked the Company nominal roll, we have several unaccounted for. We must ask something more of you before we finish here. Not yet however. Get some rest and hot food. Once A Company has finished on task, we know what we have to do."

With that he turned to Justin, who by the looks of things was trying his hardest to hold it together. Dale took him gently by the arm and led him in to the rocks a little way from us. B Company had taken a real battering, and he just needed some fatherly reassurance from his Company Sergeant Major, the most seasoned soldier in his Company, that his plan and decisions were the right course of action. They settled down with the remainder of his group, which among the rocks was nothing more than a series of helmets and radio antennas bobbing around. Gunfire and the thud of grenades continued further along the mountain as A Company took care of business. I'm sure it wouldn't be long before they would start ferrying more of their guys back to the RAP. We couldn't make out who was doing the shooting and grenade lobbing; the enemy could be counter-attacking for all we knew. The only indication of who was doing the damage was you could tell a trained soldier from the short controlled bursts of a machine gun, and the wild erratic long bursts of an amateur. Not much else. There was plenty of shouting and screaming up on the feature, but you couldn't make out if it was English or Spanish. Before long, the fighting had petered out to the odd burst of gunfire and thud of grenades.

Dale emerged from his perch among the rocks, and called for our attention.

"Guys, let's do this. All Platoons will back track their route here and carefully make your way up your original routes, checking bunkers and any dead you encounter, including enemy. Take caution however. Some sneaky bastards may have booby trapped the dead, theirs and ours. You are to keep out of sight of Tumbledown to the South, which is still occupied. Some of em may emerge from bunkers we missed in the advance and surrender, so be on your game, understand?"

We nodded, and began to get our gear on, Dale waved his arms.

"Weapons and smocks only, belts and mags ready to use."

Happy with that.

I handed Jamie back his waterproof, confident I would find the barrel bag, and my precious warm kit. I had a belt of about fifty rounds on the gun, and I wrapped another two hundred around me just in case we encountered trouble. We began to move out, 4 Platoon leading, then us, and what was left of 6 was behind us. Company HQ stayed where it was for now. It wasn't long before 4 skirted up and around to the left into the alleys, where they had the grim task of carving the enemy out of their stronghold. Despite the fog, the early morning light made identifying features and positions much easier. Most of the bunkers 4 had dealt with in the night were still smouldering from their destruction with grenades, both High Explosive, and White Phosphorous. We continued past them and around the large rock slabs that divided the mountain like a large toast rack. It wasn't long before we could see the ground we cleared in the darkness. Smouldering bunkers marked our progress. We passed closely on our left side a bunker that had a caved in timber roof. My stomach turned over when it quickly dawned on me. This was the bunker I fell in. Jamie knelt down on the edge of it and inhaled.

"Wow, something is cooking a treat in there."

What was cooking would be the two guys I fell on. It could have been so different if they were ready for me as I came crashing through their roof. Davo called for our attention.

"Guys, break down into pairs, and check all the positions you can find. Any dead you encounter, check them too, remember to look out for booby traps, no funny stuff."

Everyone spread out, Jamie and I stayed put. I turned my back to the bunker, trying to retrace my route to the barrel bag. There was a series of rock clusters between us and the open ground where we had our Start Line. We made our way between the rock clusters and found evidence of last night's fighting. Webbing, brass casings, medical kit. No bodies however. This may have been the first pieces of cover for the Company when it all kicked off. Before we ended up in the open ground we both stopped. I turned around and faced back up the mountain. In the morning light, it didn't look as steep as it did in the darkness. It felt like we were fighting our way up a cliff face during the night. I looked over to my right and saw another cluster of rocks, and made our way to it. On one side of the rocks were some fresh empty cases and some belt link from a machine gun. This must be it. A little way out from the rocks was a sorry looking canvas bag, shredded beyond use. My barrel bag. I rummaged through it. Everything in it had been badly battered. The spare barrels were chipped beyond use; my quilted suit didn't look fit to go on a scarecrow. My waterproofs were half shredded, and half melted to the barrels. What bastards shot fuck out of my kit? I was too cold to be fussy at this point, my army woollen jersey didn't look too bad, and I wasted no time getting it on. Straight away, having another layer on was pure bliss. I didn't care for its appearance, it would be under my smock, and therefore Dale wouldn't spot it, and chew me out for my trampish appearance. I took the remainder of the barrel bag, and slung it over my back. It would have to do. We then began to slowly make our way up the feature and help the guys search for dead and wounded.

As we picked our way through the rocks we saw up ahead a few of the guys stood over what could only be a bunker or something. As we pulled up next to them, a horror show lay at our feet. We had found the Boss and what appeared to be Kyle. I could feel the burning bile as it tried to rise up into my mouth, but I managed to keep it down. Both had been riddled with bullet holes, and grenade splinters. They had passed bleeding out; their blood had soaked through their clothing and the peat around them. The way they had met their deaths was clear to see. Tony was on his back with his smock and shirt open, with what appeared to be a horrific chest wound, and Kyle was slumped over his midriff, hands full of field dressings, clearly trying to save his Platoon Commanders life. Their bodies had clearly been caught in the crossfire of soldiers fighting in the darkness. Tony's helmet had been smashed by a number of rounds, but yet his face remained intact. Kyle had not been so lucky. He had taken entry wounds through the face that appeared clean, but the back of his helmet was missing, along with the contents of his head, giving the appearance of a scooped out egg shell. We just stood there taking in the scene. Davo broke our silence.

"Get Kyle's poncho, and cover them over. Mark their position with one of their rifles."

We looked at each other for a moment, none of us wanting to touch them. Davo rolled his eyes and knelt down behind Kyle.

"For fuck sake", he cursed under his breath, loud enough for us to hear.

He undid Kyle's canvas roll on top of his webbing pouches and began to unwrap his poncho. I then took this as my cue to pick up one of their weapons and point it muzzle down in the peat deep enough for it to stand unaided. Jamie and Leighton helped Davo spread out the poncho and drape it over the bodies, Davo then held up his hand.

"Wait, ammo, water and rations, they don't need them anymore."

This is not what I had in mind, but he was right, we needed these precious commodities now. I knelt down behind Kyle, and went through his pouches. I found six full magazines for his rifle, including the one I removed from his weapon, two water bottles that were almost full, and a mixed bag of sweets, brew kit, and biscuits. We couldn't get to the Boss's kit in his webbing, but Davo made it his task to go through his smock for his map and compass. Once done, we placed the poncho over them and weighed the corners down with whatever rocks or ballast was available to hand.

"Let's check the rest of the area", Davo ordered, "we can come back for these guys later."

We then made our way further up the feature towards the top of the saddle, and it was then I saw what the enemy looked like up close, and somewhat dead. This one particular bunker we discovered had a couple of olive drab tents partially collapsed behind it. You couldn't see the tents until you were right on top of the position, since they had been concealed and protected by a series of large rocks. In front of the bunker entrance itself was two bodies in olive drab quilted jackets, olive drab denims, but no boots or socks. These guys were completely riddled with bullet holes, large dried blood patches underneath them where they had bled out all over the peat. One of them had a radio handset clutched in one hand and rosary in the other. The other was lying on top of what looked like his own personal weapon, but a magazine in his right hand. These guys must have been fighting when our lads piled into their protected campsite. The tents behind them were as sorry site. Both tents were riddled with bullet holes and grenade splinters. The right tent still held its unfortunate occupants, killed in the dark whilst still in their sleeping bags. One of them had attempted to scramble out the back end of the tent, half out of his sleeping bag, half dressed, and his face caved in by heavy gunfire. The left tent appeared unoccupied, but blood was evident around its base. Maybe these guys had survived the assault and had escaped, away from the carnage. This position had been destroyed by our guys with extreme violence. Jamie went forward, and without ceremony prodded the bodies with the muzzle of his rifle. Dead for sure.

There was a clatter of metal to our left and we could see a pale hand waving at us from a small hole in amongst the rocks and peat. Weapons at the ready, we formed a base line and faced the hand. Then there appeared the green dome of a helmet, then a pale face. Davo took a step forward and pointed his weapon at the face.

"Out, NOW!" he growled," Get the fuck out or we will shoot."

Another hand now appeared. This person then shuffled his shoulders through the gap and revealed his torso. He then scrambled out quickly so his feet were clear and rolled on his back with his hands in the air. Our first prisoner. Davo stormed over to the hole with us covering the guy on the floor, and began to demand that anyone else in the hole surrender. Nothing. He clicked his fingers at the guy on the floor to get his attention, who very quickly got the gist of what Davo was about to do. Davo had pulled a grenade from a pouch, and made it clear he was going to frag the hole. The prisoner then ranted something loudly in Spanish towards the hole over and over. Movement and commotion could now be heard in the hole. Our prisoner kept shouting at the hole. Another pair of hands appeared out of the hole, followed by a mop of black, greasy hair. Davo had put the grenade back in his pouch at this point, and leaned in and grabbed this second person by the scruff of the neck, dragging them out, gagging and choking as he pulled him alongside the other one. Davo returned to the hole. Was there anymore? One of the enemy soldiers waved his hands, no more, this was it. Davo was clear on what he wanted to happen next.

"Archie, cover them, Zane, Jamie search them, now."

Leighton moved over to Davo, who was preparing a grenade for the follow up. He pulled the pin and in it went. A few seconds later, there was a loud thud, followed by smoke drifting from the hole. Jamie and Zane went to work searching our prisoners, both lying flat on their backs, arms out stretched. The lads were abit hesitant to start with, but soon got their groove, and checking them over methodically. Watch, wallet with a few photos of family, a rosary, some cigarettes, nothing that led us to believe they were of any importance on this position, just two conscripts hoping not to get killed today. Well their luck was in. Zane got to his feet.

"Nothing, no maps or command kit, just soldiers."

We looked up the mountain, and saw the remainder of the Platoon having the same experience as us. Enemy soldiers began to appear out of the slimmest of gaps in the rocks. They must have sat tight and silent through last night, praying they wouldn't be discovered. Since the largest group of prisoners was above us, we pulled our two to their feet and moved them up to join their comrades. As we arrived, the other group of prisoners was laying face down, side by side with their hands on their heads. We put our two on the left end of the line and they copied the others.

"Gunners stay here and watch these lot"; Davo called out," the remainder keep searching."

Being a gunner, I got babysitting duty whilst the lads went further up the feature searching for our dead, and with abit of luck, maybe some wounded. I looked over to where the remainder of our Platoon gathered.

They were stood around the bodies of the two guys that knocked out the problem bunker in the night. From what I could see, they carefully laid the sitting body down on its side carefully, as if not to wake him, and as for the guy in front, he was almost burnt to a cinder. Ponchos and blankets appeared and two rifles placed muzzle down in the ground to mark them as ours. Up out of the rocks to the right, what appeared to be 6 Platoon came into view and amongst them, a handful of prisoners. They placed their prisoners onto our line on the right side. Not including 4 Platoon, B Company had a fair size bag of prisoners. If all these had put up a fight last night, some of us stood around guarding them could have been under a blanket marked with a rifle. Below us, appeared two figures, as they drew near, we made out the profiles of Dale and Justin. As they pulled up, Dale let out a whistle.

"Fucking hell boys, look at this lot."

"How is 4 getting on?" Asked one of the 6 Platoon lads.

"They've got a couple," Justin answered, "and they are wounded, no one else, I don't think 4 were in the mood to be nice last night."

"Right guys," Dale cut in, "lets not bite off more than we can chew, get these fuckers down to the RAP."

Just as he finished talking, there was a high pitched screech as shell fire smashed all over the top of the saddle, we scattered in amongst the rocks around us, the prisoners stayed where they were, squirming uncomfortably, wanting the shelling to finish. Heavy shell fire smashed the saddle and the backside of the feature, really making the ground beneath us shudder. Shell fire thudded and smashed into the open ground just in front of our Start Line from last night. It last but a few minutes, but seemed much longer. Once it had finished, we carefully emerged from our cover, the prisoners were crying and squirming nonstop.

"They have lost this position." Justin announced proudly, "That's their defensive fire plan, shell their own positions, and deny it to us."

"Beautiful, just what I always wanted." an anonymous voice from amongst the 6 Platoon lads.

There was some nervous giggling amongst our boys, they began to pull the prisoners to their feet and lead them off the feature down and around to the RAP. I didn't want to lead, so I hung back until the prisoners began to be shepherded down the mountain. Davo hung back next to me, looking at me like he wanted to say something.

"We found Danny and John and Brandon." He murmured.

"Where?"

He didn't answer, just flicked his eyes to the position with the sitting body.

"Shit, really? Who?" I couldn't get my words out straight.

"Danny was the one sitting, John was the one that caught fire, Brandon and two enemies are in the bunker, it's real messy in there." He looked so sad, he began to well up.

I was stunned for words; three platoon characters killed dealing with one bunker, fuck.

"We will come back for them, once we've dealt with these prisoners, don't want to be overstretched just in case they counter attack." He managed to compose himself, and it was business as usual.

As we drew just short of the RAP, A Company were already bringing in their prisoners and O.B called out for ours to join the others. Our prisoners were dropped off with some of what I believe to be A Company lads who were assigned to guard them. Some prisoners were now bringing in their dead, piled up without ceremony in front of where they were told to sit, and this all made for grim viewing. The dead appeared to be like department store dummies, badly dressed. Their uniforms hanging off them were revealing the grim nature of their deaths. Bullet holes, grenade splinters, bayonet puncture wounds. Some were missing heads altogether, their jackets soaked black with their blood. What I found most bizarre, was the fact that most of the dead had no boots on, or were in just a shirt and trousers. Were these guys caught half dressed in their positions? Fighting and dying in what they slept in? This grim sight was not what I was expecting, I had this romantic image in my tiny mind of dying with blazing guns to an awesome soundtrack, not getting my head blown off or bayoneted in the face whilst struggling to get out of my sleeping bag.

We then moved into the clump of rocks we had established ourselves in before Dale sent us out to account for missing people. I found my webbing, and dumped my poor excuse of a barrel bag next to it. Dale came over to me.

"What the hell happened to that?" he enquired. I came clean.

"I took it off at my first piece of cover Sir, and it got fragged."

He shook his head, and chuckled.

"Well Archie boy, just think, if you'd been wearing it when it got the good news, we'd be covering you with a poncho."

Shit, he had a point.

"Is your warm kit shagged?" he pursued.

"Yes Sir and it's not getting any warmer."

This wasnt far from the truth, the early morning fog had all but disappeared revealing a brilliant but freezing cold sky.

"Well" he looked at the pile of enemy dead, and then looked at me with a serious glare, "you won't have to go too far to shop for new stuff, will you?"

I just looked at him, hoping he wasn't serious.

"Lets be clear on this Archie, they don't need it anymore, do they?"

Holy shit.

With that, he walked off. I sat down, stunned. Jamie came and sat with me, digging into his webbing for his brew kit. Without waiting for me to offer, he leant over and pulled out my Hot Chocolate, and one of my water bottles. I started to shiver, it was getting colder, with the activity of the last hour or so, my body began to cool down again. Jamie rabbited away, and you know what? I wasn't listening to a word of it. I just looked at my hands, and then the pile of bodies, than back at my hands. Jamie jabbed me in the arm, which snapped me out of my own world.

"Are you ignoring me?" he demanded.

"What?"

"I said, do you want me to cook you some scoff?" He rolled his eyes.

"Yeah, cheers." I dug into one of my webbing pouches and threw him a bag of instant porridge.

"What did Dale say? Did he give you a bollocking for the barrel bag?"

I looked at the sorry looking barrel bag, and it dawned on me Dale wasn't really that interested in it.

"No, he asked if my warm kit was still in good shape and if not where to get some."

"Where to get some?" Jamie quizzed "The Quartermaster is at Estancia."

He then looked at the pile of bodies, and then back at me, his smile quickly disappeared quickly to become a look of horror. He didn't say anything else; he looked down and took great interest in our porridge on the burner. We sat in silence while the water came to the boil, neither of us wanting to talk about what Dale had implied. Jamie then raised his head, lips pursed as he began to talk when a high pitched thunder roared over the mountain, and thumped into the open ground to the North of us. Shells smashed into the summit, and further along the feature amongst A Company's positions. For every shell that smashed into the mountain, two would thud out in the open ground. It became clear, the RSM had sited the RAP well, the shelling would not hit us directly, but it didn't make you any more comfortable to be shelled in the first place. The prisoners all huddled in together, hands on their ears, since the noise and concussion was immense. Being shelled is one thing, being shelled by your own side is a real shit day at the office. We turned over onto our bellies either side of our breakfast that was almost ready to be eaten. Every now and again, we'd have to hold the mess tin in place so the vibration of the explosions wouldn't ruin our efforts. The shelling ended as soon as it started. Once the echo of the explosions faded away, we could hear calls for medics up on the mountain, someone was hurt, didn't know which side, at this time, we were all in the same boat.

10

Above us on the mountain was some commotion. Casualties from the last period of shelling were being dealt with and getting brought down into the RAP. It was starting to get rather crowded, and with that Dale came to a decision.

"B Company listen up. If you are not wounded, move back up onto the feature so room can be made down here for those that need it. Locate decent cover so you've got somewhere to go when they shell us again, which they probably will. Get your gear and don't go any further east of the bowl. Move now."

We got to our feet, and started pulling our gear on. Jamie grabbed my arm.

"Let's go do this, so we don't have to come back down here again."

With that we made our way over to the pile of enemy dead. None of them looked pretty; the cause of their demise was clear to see. Jamie began to strip off his gear as three prisoners arrived dragging one of their dead by the ankles. Two had hold of the ankles, dragging the body as if they didn't have a care in the world. I think I can safely say our dead were not being dragged to the RAP in that manner. The body was naked from the waist up, and without a head. The third prisoner was carrying the missing body part, cradling it in his arms, his face void of any emotion. They didn't try to put it on the pile, they just left it along side it, the head placed on top facing the pile. Grim.

The prisoners made their way over to where the group of prisoners were sat. Jamie began to circle the pile, checking out what was on special offer. I was after one of their duvet jackets; they looked the business, with as minimal evidence of its previous owner as possible. I took my fighting gear off and began to look more into what the dead were wearing. Pickings were slim; the jackets I was interested in were in real bad shape. I couldn't wear a jacket soaked in blood, brain, and snot of its former owner, not only is it a serious moral issue, but clearly not hygienic. Jamie let out a whistle.

"What about this one?"

I moved around the pile and at his feet was a potential candidate. The body was free of blood, so it appeared, fully dressed, and in fairly good shape. One could only imagine what had killed him and with minimal damage. His arms were outstretched, giving the impression he had been frozen solid trying to strangle someone. Strange. We took hold of his jacket and trouser legs and turned him on his side to inspect the back, no damage there. I was puzzled.

"What the fuck happened to him?" I said out loud.

"Blast" came a voice on the other side of the pile, "probably naval gunfire."

We both scrambled to our feet, only to see Dale stood over the other side.

"O.B said to be quick about it and fuck off, before you get lynched by that lot."

We looked over his shoulder to see our prisoners getting rather irate about our interest in their dead comrades, the lads guarding them started to get heavy handed with them to sit down and be quiet.

"We have a jacket" Jamie piped up, "its not going to be easy getting it off without some reshaping if you get my drift."

"Get on with it", Dale demanded through gritted teeth.

Without hesitation, Jamie pushed me to one side, and stamped on the right arm of the body, resulting in an almighty crack. I turned away as my stomach turned over spraying the ground beneath me with porridge and hot chocolate, that all too familiar burning sensation in full force in my throat and mouth. Why did you do that Jamie? I then heard another crack as Jamie continued with his method of straightening dead men's arms.

"Help me then for fuck sake, it's your bloody jacket" he barked as he pulled the body onto its front.

I helped him get it turned over, Jamie then stood back up both hands clutching the jacket and his right boot firmly between the shoulder blades of its current owner. I felt rather faint. A few seconds later the jacket was free. Jamie slung it at me as he jogged back to his kit. I didn't examine the goods straight away, I followed Jamie, getting kitted up in quick time and walking briskly over to where Davo and the other lads had gathered at the entrance of the bowl.

As we entered the bowl, it was clear to see how brutal the fighting had been in here. We had the luxury of being sat up high, firing down and across in support of the lads clearing the bunkers. But down in the bowl itself, told a whole different story. There were bodies everywhere, theirs, and ours. A Company were still clearing out a few stubborn defenders to the east of the bowl, and had yet to come and deal with their dead. I hope we didn't get spammed with clearing them, since we still had to recover our own. The first bunker I encountered had collapsed; its occupants were crushed under the weight of a huge slab of rock that had been its roof. An Argentine soldier was half hanging out of the position, right arm outside and his head were visible, his jaw crushed with dried blood and snot congealed all over the rock he was slumped over. In front of the bunker on the grass was the body of one of ours, face down, fully kitted up, and riddled with bullets and grenade splinters. I didn't know the guy, but he was a member of the Battalion nonetheless. We started to climb the bowl towards where we were during the night giving fire support, over to our left was the smouldering bunker that cost the lives of the three that tried to storm it. One was still propped up by his rifle, his body smashed beyond recognition having been caught in a furious crossfire. Lying next to him was the headless remains of his mate who got a face full of machine gun fire, and across the opening of the bunker itself was the lower half of another whose grenades were hit and blew him in half. Dried blood and internal organs were scattered over the rocks to the left of the bunker entrance.

One could only imagine what was left of the occupants of that position, when the rather pissed off lads of A Company came to silence that position for good. Jamie and I found a relatively flat piece of ground just below the upper rim of the bowl. Not too sure how much cover it would give us from the shelling but I didn't want to get into the bunkers, not knowing what state they were in inside. I took my gear off and sat on my webbing. With my back to the rocks I had one hell of a view of the carnage that had taken place here in the dark. It wasn't long before the cold began to creep in again, and I examined my newly acquired duvet jacket. Jamie had chosen well, it was in good condition, but reeked of body odour. Its former owner must have put it on in Argentina and hadn't taken it off since, it smelt vile. The cold air kept me from being too proud to wear it, and I put it on. It did fit rather nicely and with the zip done up all the way up to my chin, it certainly kept the cold out, and the foul odour inside. Beggars can't be choosers.

As I leaned forward to adjust my seating position, I felt something digging into my right side. Undoing the zip and getting a fresh face full of dried sweat, I discovered an inside pocket. I put my hand in, and felt what had the texture of paper and plastic. I pulled the items out to discover they were letters and a couple of laminated photos. The letters were in Spanish, so therefore didn't have a clue what they said. They had a very mild scent of perfume, probably letters from a girlfriend. The two photos were of a rather attractive young girl, probably the author of the letters, and what I could only guess was his family prior to his departure on this crusade to reassert Argentine pride. This young soldier in the photo was stood in the centre of the shot with possibly his family flanking him. All looking very proud of their son or brother doing his duty for his country. If only they knew he was now on a pile of badly smashed corpses, after having his life ripped from him by the blast of Artillery. Looted of his clothing by enemy soldiers who now enjoyed the warmth his jacket provided and looking through his personal effects. If the roles were reversed, it would shatter my Mum and Dad.

A small group of prisoners came into the lower part of the bowl, escorted by a couple of our guys. They made their way over to the first bodies in their way. The bodies were a mixture of theirs and ours, and judging by the way they were laid out, it was gruesome hand to hand fighting, a real fight to the death. They were probably cut down in the frenzied fire fight as A Company attempted to rush the positions in the darkness. I watched with interest as the prisoners carefully moved our dead to one side, probably fearing swift justice from their guards should they be disrespectful, but would then grab the ankles of their own dead and without ceremony, drag them towards the RAP, truly bizarre. Was this the way they dealt with their dead as a matter of course, or were they just a large group of strangers told to defend this mountain? I looked at the letters and photos in my hands; I didn't want to keep these as trophies. I got to my feet, leaving all my kit with Jamie, who in typical fashion had a brew on the go; I jogged down the slope and caught the attention of our guys guarding them. I walked up to the nearest prisoner, pulled his jacket open, and stuffed the letters and photos in his pocket. With that, I gave him a friendly jab in his shoulder, and in return he gave me a slight grin and a nod. I turned on my heels and made my way back up to Jamie, hoping the soldier would look at the effects later, and understand what I wanted him to do. They shouldn't end up in a mass grave. Get them home.

I sat back down on my perch, and Jamie passed the brew to me, Coffee.

"Out of chocolate mate, Coffee it is" he grinned.

I wasn't bothered; I cupped it in my hands, enjoying the warmth, sipping it slowly. Below us, Davo and some of the guys were inspecting the bunkers, and even venturing into them. It became apparent what they discovered, when whoever went in poked their head back out to vomit, which the remainder found rather entertaining. It quickly began to dawn on me how tired I was. The warmth of the coffee and my new jacket made me drowsy; the adrenaline fuelled night had drained from me as I began to relax. A rather bizarre sensation considering the environment we were in right now, hardly serene. Freezing cold, death everywhere you looked, smouldering bunkers that reeked of human shit, the smell of cordite from fired ammunition, one hell of a day at the office.

What appeared to be our guys, by that I mean A Company lads, appeared in the bowl. Each of them had some kind of white sleeping bag tucked under their arms. What on earth was it? They stood over their dead and between them began to unfold this white object. The penny dropped as soon as they laid it alongside their dead comrade, body bags. They laid it flat next to the body, and between them, they carefully lifted it, with other guys sliding the bag underneath. Once they lowered the body, they folded the body bag flap over it and zipped it up, done. Four of them each grabbed a corner and made their way down and out of the bowl, probably towards the RAP. The same group of lads appeared in the bowl a short while later to repeat the process for another one of their dead. This continued for some time, the last of which were the propped up body and the grim remains of his two mates who tried to knock their target bunker out. I was expecting Dale to appear and round us up for the same task with our own dead, but he hadn't, maybe that task was already in hand with the manpower he had around him. I just hoped he didn't come looking for extra muscle, I don't think I could face the task of shovelling what was left of Brandon out of that bunker which killed John and Danny also. I recalled it reeking of shit when we passed it in the night. Call me callous if you like, but I was not going to volunteer for the task.

Jamie watched the whole scene below us with a dead pan expression, everything we had been exposed to during the last twelve or so hours he took without so much of a whimper. The comedian in him had not made an appearance since we left Estancia for our assembly area on Mount Vernet. He wasn't shy with getting to grips with the bodies when finding me some warm kit, and there's me puking all over the shop. I was getting abit worried about Jamie, he wasn't himself. He appeared emotionless to everything we'd done so far, not happy go lucky, just business. What did I know? Maybe it was the best way to deal with things right now. I just hoped he snapped out of it when it was all over. He peered over to me, about to speak when he paused, his eyes narrowed to a glare,

"What the fuck is that on the front of your helmet?"

I peeled the helmet off my head and inspected the front. It was smeared in what could only be described as a light pink mush with dark hair stuck in amongst the black tape and camo. It smelt vile. I could only guess it was the remains of the soldier's face I head butted repeatedly in the bunker I fell in. My stomach turned over, but I had nothing to bring up, so all I had to deal with was the bile burning my throat, which I managed to keep down. I promptly grabbed the helmet with both hands and rubbed the front of it on the peat and grass next to me.

Jamie pressed,

"What happened when we got split last night?"

I kept my eyes focused on the helmet,

"I fell into a bunker; there were two of them in their sleeping bags."

I glanced up; Jamie had a wicked grin on his face,

"Totally awesome, what did you do?"

Jamie you bastard.

"I shot the first one, but the other was in my face before I knew it. I head butted him again and again until he stopped moving, that's it."

"Cool", Jamie was impressed.

"Dale dragged me out the trench and finished them off with a white phos".

Jamie chuckled,

"That's fucking hardcore mate, good for you".

Really?

Our conversation was cut short by commotion above and behind us. We both stood up and turned to see what was causing the noise. Just behind the rocks we were peering over was a group of Argentine soldiers along with a couple of ours gathered around in a tight group looking at the ground. Jamie and I scrambled up to a better vantage point. On the ground at the feet of the group was what appeared to be a wounded Argentine soldier being tended to by one of our medics. We clambered up to assist; it quickly dawned on me where exactly we were. We were at the top of the alleys we fought our way up last night. We must have missed this guy in the darkness as we scrambled forward to support A Company in the bowl.

Evidence of our presence here last night was clear to see, brass cases and spent link all over the place. I took in our surroundings, off to the east in the far distance was what I could only guess was Port Stanley. Our ultimate prize. Not the sprawling metropolis I had in my head, but the islands capital all the same. I panned right and the full imposing feature of Mount Tumbledown loomed over us across the wide valley. I glanced over to where the group remained in place; they had got their casualty ready to travel.

"Get off the fucking top, NOW!"

I looked down to see Dale staring straight up at us, with others in attendance, empty body bags at their feet. As I quickly mustered the words in my tiny brain to justify our bold action, the roars of shells smashing into the cliffs above the alleys rendering me deaf in a high pitch whine of ringing eardrums. As I dropped to the ground, I could just make out the muffled screams of casualties and people shouting "incoming." The casualty lying on the ground, flinching wildly as shell splinters smashed into him and the ground around him. The concussion of the shells burst his head like a tomato as a near miss rocked us. I peered over the rock in front of me as shells smashed into the rocks above us and thudded into the peat on the exposed summit. Our medic was crawling towards me, his face all bloody, and his right leg a mangled mess. Off to the right, one of the Argentine soldiers broke cover and dashed over to him. Just as he reached him another shell burst in the open ground just off to his right. Without ceremony, he grabbed our guy and dragged him into cover, madness. The shelling ended as suddenly as it began. I raised my head a little higher and peered over to where I last saw Jamie. He looked back at me with thumbs up, thank heavens. The gorse and peat on the summit had caught fire and smouldered badly. As my hearing returned I could make out someone calling my name out behind me. I turned around and looked into the bowl. It was Dale.

"Let me know what you need, and we will get it up to you."

My head was still swimming, as I gave myself a moment to gather my thoughts and shit together. I got myself into the kneeling position, not confident about admiring the view anymore. The prisoners and their guards emerged from whatever cover they found during the shelling. This time however, they had one of ours to deal with, the medic. To their credit, they got him ready to move in quick time, under the direction of the Argentine who dashed out and saved him. He was jabbering away in Spanish, physically gripping his comrades, who were just sobbing wrecks of men. They lifted our man and began the slow and treacherous decent into the bowl, on route to the RAP. Jamie and I assisted with taking the weight of our man, as they crossed the more technical parts of the climb down over the lip. Once down onto better ground, Dale then took over the casevac, which left Jamie and I to return to our gear just below the lip. As we sat down, Dale called out to us.

"Stay off the fucking top, do you hear me?"

We nodded.

With that, he moved off down the bowl following the group carrying the wounded medic. As he drew level with the rear man, who just happened to be a prisoner, he lurched out and grabbed him just as he stumbled and feel to his knees, and then slumped onto his back. We just sat there, not really sure what had just taken place. Dale appeared to be stood wide legged over him, who then look straight at us and unleashed his rarely seen fury,

"Don't just fucking sit there, get here now!"

We were legging it down towards the Company Sergeant Major in a flash, struggling to sling our weapons as we ran. As we pulled up, Dale was tearing at the prisoners clothing. I recognized the guy straight away. It was the prisoner who saved our medic.

"Quick, look for wounds, anything."

We scrambled to get his jacket open, shirt open. No sign of blood or wound. Dale pulled out his clasp knife from his smock and cut the man's belt, frantically pulling down his trousers, blood. He then cut free the man's soiled underwear. The man's groin was a mass of smeared blood and shit. Dale used the guy's underwear to wipe the vile grime away as best he could, in an attempt to find the wound. Nothing.

"Roll him over" he barked at us.

We flipped the guy over, more blood and shit smeared all over his buttocks. Still couldn't find the wound. Dale then grabbed the man's trousers by the crutch which was dark with blood and yanked them down to the point where they couldn't get over his boots.

"Part his legs, now!"

Jamie and I scrambled to get this guy's legs open, hands slippery with blood, revealing his penis and testicles. Just to the right of his testicles we found a puncture wound, half an inch wide and about two inches long. Blood pumped out in a rhythm which could only mean one thing, the femoral artery. Dale pulled from his smock pocket a field dressing, and ripped off the packaging.

"Sir," Jamie piped up, "we are going to need more than one".

"Fuck the wound", he growled, "tourniquet, help me make it tight".

This guy was groaning and delirious with both pain and blood loss. We flipped him onto his back and promptly lifted the guy's legs so Dale could wrap the dressing above the wound, in towards the groin. Once in the right place, Dale pulled it fucking tight, to stop the bleeding. The blood seeped out slightly from the wound, it must have been tight.

Dale used one of his blood smeared fingers to write the letter "T" on the man's forehead. He glanced at his watch and then wrote the time just below it. The "T" would indicate to medics and surgeons further down the CASEVAC chain that a tourniquet was fitted, should the casualty be wrapped up warm, and the time let them know what time it was fitted. Simple yet effective. Jamie then fished a dressing from his smock and then took care to dress the wound so it wouldn't get filled with mud and shit during the journey to the RAP. As Jamie had finished, others had arrived and quickly got the guy into a poncho and dragged him away down out of the bowl, leaving us and Dale sat on our own amid blood soaked peat and dressing packaging. Dale pulled off his helmet, and wiped his brow with the back of a blood smeared hand.

"I think he will lose the leg." He commented.

"That was the guy that saved our medic". I observed.

Dale didn't answer. He wiped his hands on the grass around him. Looked up at the sky, I could see his eyes were now glazed with both emotion and exhaustion. Before he let his guard down altogether, he put his helmet back on, and got to his feet, straightening himself up. Back to business.

"Grab your gear and get back to the RAP, the O.C will brief the company on the next phase of operations."

We nodded.

He turned and made his way down out of the bowl. Next phase? Really? I wasn't sure if I had enough left in me to do much more at this stage. We hadn't slept since yesterday morning; any food I took in would only be sprayed all over the bloody mountain at every turn in this fucking fight. We clambered to our feet, and slowly made our way back up to our kit. The short but steep climb really took it out of me, all my energy drained from the adrenaline of the last hour or so. As I reached for my webbing, I noticed my hands, covered in another man's blood, along with shit and peat. I fished out a water bottle and went to town getting as much of the foul coating off as possible. Once satisfied, I looked for something to dry my hands on. My clothing was filthy, so had to just let them dry naturally. I pulled out my leather gloves from my smock and slipped them on. I felt more confident handling food and drink with my gloves on than I would with my bare hands at this time, let's put it that way. Jamie and I struggled into our kit, once sorted, we trudged back down towards the RAP, leaving the various work parties in the bowl dealing with the dead.

As we made our way left out of the bowl, we noticed that the RAP was even busier than before, a real hive of activity. Fuck knows how, but a small helicopter was parked there along with two over-snow vehicles favoured by the Commandos. Small work parties were carrying stretchers over to the helicopter, which was nothing more than a plastics bubble, with two cocoon like boxes on the running skids. The two stretcher casualties were hustled into these boxes and once secure, the rotors would begin to turn. In next to no time, this little helicopter rose up slightly and banked away to the North hugging the ground we followed as we approached this mountain the night before. I take it the more seriously wounded got the helicopter ride out of here, since what I could make out as walking wounded were getting bundled into the snow vehicles.

Over to our left, amongst the rocks was a large group of prisoners that had survived the night and had surrendered when the time was right. They looked filthy, exhausted, and bloody young. They all had their hoods up and hands in their pockets, shivering uncontrollably. To be honest, we fared no better, it was the training we had that got us through I think. Off to the right was the grim view of their dead. The pile was bigger, still exposed to the elements; many of them had their eyes open, staring straight back at us and their surviving comrades. It reminded me of pictures of Auschwitz and others like it. Whatever the generation, whatever the war, close combat is savage and grim, plain and simple.

Further along, we came across the wounded, theirs and ours. They were all mixed together with medics, both theirs and ours, beavering away to get them patched up and as comfortable as possible. Most were sat in amongst the rocks, trying to keep warm wrapped in blankets and sleeping bags that looked like they had seen better days. Some looked in a real bad way, others just sat there passing the time of day with a cigarette hanging from their lips. The seriously wounded, were on stretchers, heavily wrapped in blankets with some of their comrades or a medic holding up a saline drip for them. The law of the land was no matter what side you fought for, if you were a serious case, you went first. Some humanity had to surface in this god awful place. There was one of our guys, possibly the Medical Officer, dishing out instructions to the medics, either in English or terrible Spanish, he had a notebook in his gloved paws, placing casualties in priority order for the ride out of here. Despite the grim setting, it all looked rather organised.

We continued on a short distance and found some familiar faces in amongst the rocks, B Company, what was left of it. The numbers were fewer than there was earlier in the day. Maybe the shelling was the cause of it; I didn't have the bottle to ask anyone. Archie, just find a spot and shut up! Jamie and I found a patch to settle in, took off our gear and sat on it. My newly acquired duvet jacket turned a few heads, not sure if it was the novelty factor or the smell; it was still ripe with its former owner's fragrance. Davo stood up a short distance away and waved me over. I got to my feet and made my way over. He led me a short distance from the lads.

"Archie, get that jacket under your smock, the prisoners are not happy with the fact we've been taking boots and shit off their dead. Any press sniffing around in Stanley will have a field day with this shit, get it sorted".

"Sure thing Davo, sorry".

"Don't sweat it mate, we've all got jackets and boots, their gear is far better than ours, just don't display the fucker, alright?"

"Sure thing, thanks for the heads up".

I was correcting my state of dress when Davo nudged my arm and pointed over to O.B and Dale. At their feet was a long line of filled body bags which judging by O.B and Dale consulting their notebooks meant they were B Company dead. Further along was another line of body bags with another character stood over them, notebook at the ready. He must have been A Company's Sergeant Major. I didn't know his name, I was too junior for one thing, and you tended to just socialise with your own company most of the time anyway. The names of those that had been killed were clear to see in bold black marker pen, written on the side. Among them were the Boss, Danny, John, Brandon and Kyle. That was just from our Platoon; the remainder were made up from 4 and 6 Platoon. I counted 23 bags in total, a heavy price for such a prize, this bloody mountain. Not as heavy a price as the Argentines had paid; at a guess their pile of dead was about 40 odd. The cost in wounded was pretty outrageous, on both sides. I couldn't even guess what the number of wounded was, since some had already been evacuated. I observed the work parties helping the walking wounded over to the snow vehicles, their war over, on the way to the rear for treatment. How far rear? Estancia? Teal? San Carlos? The main thing was they were getting the hell out of here.

11

The RAP was slowly emptying of wounded as the helicopter and snow-vehicles ferried them out of here. All around where we were sat you could smell various aromas, human shit, the coppery tang of blood, hexamine tablets, various hot food, burnt peat, cordite from spent ammunition, a real treat for the nasal senses. I chose to eat with my gloves on since eating with my bare hands was not a healthy option. Dale came over to me and Jamie and threw us some sterile wipes and what looked like toothpicks.

"Got these from the Medical Officer, for your hands."

"Thanks Sir, nice one"

He went about his business, as Jamie and I went to town on our hands, swabbing them down and scraping all the crud from under our fingernails. At one point it looked like we wouldn't have enough, but we soon made progress with our ablutions. With our hands all clean it then dawned on me that the inside of my gloves was now a bio hazard in the making. I stuffed them in my smock, only when my fingers were on the verge of frostbite would they go back on. I then tucked into my food confident my hands were good enough, as I was ravenous, the beef stew and hard tack biscuits didn't touch the sides.

Once fed, we just sat on our kit watching the world go by. Another salvo screamed in and smashed all over the summit and thumped into the open ground near our Start Line. When it all calmed down, it was clear we were all ok, because no fresh wounded or dead came into the RAP. I glanced at my watch, it was mid afternoon by this stage and I was shattered. I rested my head on my forearms in an attempt to doze, but the cold was seeping through my clothing, and the odd shell crashing into the summit woke me with a jolt every time. I lifted my heavy head and movement off to my right caught my eye. O.B was dishing out body bags to the prisoners, who reluctantly made their way over to their dead comrades to conduct a most God awful chore. I rested my head back on my forearms, since I didn't want to watch the grim action and lose my food all over again. Just off to my right both Justin and Dale stood up, let off an almighty stretch and Dale then rallied the remains of his battered company.

"Gather round guys, leave your gear where it is."

We all clambered to our feet, groaning like old men, and shuffled over to where the O.C was stood. He politely asked for Platoon Commanders and Platoon Sergeants to be at the front, but all that amounted to was just a few Corporals and Davo. What a night! Justin looked rather shocked at the sight of his rather depleted chain of command. He quickly composed himself.

"Gentlemen, what was assessed as just short of Company strength defending this position in fact transpired into two Companies plus Engineer elements."

He paused to let it sink in. No wonder we had to fight for every rock on this fucking mountain. He continued.

"Information gathered from key prisoners indicates that the enemy were tasked with merely delaying us so reinforcements from Stanley and Tumbledown could then hit us from the right side. This however never took place, which I'm sure we are all pleased about."

No shit.

"Just shy of Company strength managed to disengage from us and withdraw to their reserve positions on Wireless Ridge. Brigade is more than aware of how hard our fight was last night, and has now tasked our Second Battalion with clearing Wireless Ridge tonight".

I bet they loved receiving that news.

"Second battalion are currently in a concentration area where we crossed the river. At last light they will begin their approach to their Start Line North East of here. They will have a huge amount of fire support for this tonight along with the Scots Guards going for Tumbledown, so keep this side of Longdon until further notice."

"Where do we fit into all this, Sir?" Davo asked.

"As a company, not at all. Fire Support Company is on this one. Once Wireless Ridge is secured, C Company will sweep through and clear Moody Brook Barracks, and then Advance to Contact to the racecourse just outside Stanley and take care of that bloody gun line."

How ironic, just as he referred to the enemy artillery, a lone shell smashed into the summit, making us all flinch and giggle nervously. Justin continued.

"Brigade is looking at the real possibility of street fighting, with us and Second Battalion securing the break in point, and the Commandos clearing the town, Scots Guards in reserve. The town is mostly made of wood, so it wouldn't take long before tracer and phos grenades burn the whole fucker to the ground".

More nervous tittering.

"Guys, C Company will be moving into the RAP at last light, we are to vacate here and push up into the alleys in order to make room. For those that have the idea of moving into A Company's area for a ringside seat, I would advise against it. With this shelling, decent cover are slim pickings for them, let alone us as well."

Fair point.

"Another long night tonight boys. By first light tomorrow the plan is for our forces to have the high ground overlooking Stanley, and then we can plan the break into the town itself, any questions?"

None.

Dale then took over proceedings.

"Right then, get your shit sorted, Section Commanders; get your guys up into the alleys as soon as possible, cover in there is pretty good, use the bunkers if you have to. Dismissed."

We made our way back over to our kit. Another long night lay ahead of us. If we are not involved with tonight's attacks, could we go to sleep then? I was absolutely shattered, I'm sure the whole company was chin strapped. Davo was still in conversation with Dale about something, so we just sat on our webbing until we were told to do something. It was getting colder now, my bare hands starting to feel the bite of cold. My minging gloves were last resort. I crossed my arms and wedged my hands under my armpits. It took the edge off, but not much.

Davo walked back over.

"Let's go, follow me."

What remained of our Section clambered to our feet, and we struggled back into our fighting gear. It was either getting heavier, or we were just running out of steam. Once sorted, we shuffled along behind Davo and fell into single file. We skirted left around the base of the alleys, and slowly began to climb up into them. It wasn't long before we came across the first bunkers 4 Platoon had knocked out, but Davo walked right on past and led us straight up the alley towards the top. Just short of the top, Davo turned.

"This'll do, the cover here isn't bad. If a shell gets in here, then that's just real shit luck."

I was too tired to complain, the short and sharp climb almost killed me. The duvet jacket under my smock had me hotter than hell, but it wouldn't be long before the sweat would dry and I would be a shivering wreck once again. Removing our gear, some of the lads began to explore where we had fought in the darkness. Some even attempted to scale the rock walls and check out the enemy positions. I moved up to the top of the alley where Davo and Jamie were perched. They were just eye level with the lip at the top, with the eastern end of Longdon in view and Wireless Ridge and Stanley further beyond. Flanked left and right by sheer slabs of rock, we were in reasonable cover. Should we take a shell in here any time soon, then it would simply be bad fucking luck, plain and simple.

Davo got his brew kit out and got the kettle on the go. Jamie salvaged some chocolate and biscuits from his smock and offered them around. I'd shedded my kit at this point, and got comfortable squatting on my webbing with my back against the rock wall. It became very noticeable that the whole fucking mountain reeked of human shit. Did the Argentinians just take a crap anywhere they liked? Basic sanitation did not appear to be on their list of priorities when occupying this position. Ideally you should have a latrine of sorts dug and everyone uses that, but there were turds everywhere, we could have just got plenty of kip at Estancia and just waited for the Argentinians to die of plague. Certainly the better option, considering what we had experienced last night and this morning.

What also came to my attention was that I was starting to smell abit funky with this duvet jacket on. I stripped off my smock and then unzipped the jacket. The aroma of sweat and body odour hit me in full force, which made me wretch, causing Jamie and Davo to chuckle.

"You might want to air that thing mate." Davo mused.

"Yeah, good idea."

I pulled the jacket off, pulling through the sleeves so it ended up inside out, the cold mountain air whipping around my exposed torso, which was still wrapped in my shirt and woollen jersey. I then laid it out to my left so it could air, and with abit of luck, the aroma of its former owner would vanish as well. The cold seeped into my core straight away, making me shiver. It was refreshing for a short period, but the smock was soon back on, just to take the bite off. By the time I'd finished pratting around, the brew was ready and I was handed the metal mug. It felt great with my hands wrapped around it, and upon first sip, it was a gift from the gods, Hot Chocolate.

The Hot Chocolate went around us for what seemed forever, but all too soon it was finished, and Davo had packed his gear away. There wasn't much else to do; we couldn't go on the top, and risk getting caught in the open, again. Off to the west of us we heard a distant booming sound, followed by a faint streaking noise over the top of us and faded away in the direction of Stanley. Then there would be the repeat again, but from the direction of Stanley streaking west. I looked to Davo, hoping he could shed some light on it.

"Artillery duel." He stated still looking toward Stanley. "Theirs against ours."

"Oh", that told me.

This continued for some time. Both sides trying to knock the other side out. Every now and again, one of the Argentine shells would thump into Longdon, amongst A Company's position. Probably reminding us they hadn't forgotten about us. On the horizon, the light began to fade, the cold intensifying, and our breath now very prominent in the air around us. By this stage, I couldn't handle the cold any more. The duvet jacket was back on; it smelt a little bit better.

12

It was almost dark at this point. The artillery duel had petered out, maybe both sides we now just limbering up for another night of carnage. It started to snow, light flakes of white slowly drifted across the mountain, settling on the rocks where it fell. The cold was even more intense now, the gloves becoming a more luring prospect with each passing moment. We had passed the point where we could start cooking, bearing in mind we had line of sight with whoever was occupying Wireless Ridge. The faint glow of a hexi burner could be enough for their Artillery observer on Wireless or Tumbledown to make a fine adjustment for the next salvo to come screaming in here, so it wasn't worth the risk.

In the far distance, Port Stanley was lit up for all to see. Street lights, lights on in houses, headlights moving up and down the street, without a care in the world. Truly bizarre. Right on their doorstep, troops were carving and blasting each other to bits in the mountains above them, completely bonkers. There was movement at the bottom of the alley; I could make out the shapes of a large group of soldiers. I tapped Davo on the shoulder and pointed towards them.

"C Company." He stated.

I'm glad he paid attention during the briefings.

I went back to looking at Stanley. The ultimate prize was within our grasp. Hot running water, baths and showers, beds, clean sheets, solid shelter from the weather. How many teenagers do you know, who would give these basic needs the time of day? To me at this point, they were priceless. Davo stood up and began stamping his feet, getting the blood flowing again. If it was good enough for him, when in Rome. Jamie and I followed suit. My knees creaked and my numb arse began to come back to life. Davo then rummaged through his gear and pulled out his night scope. He put it to his eye and scanned away to the north.

"Second Battalion are moving into position by the looks of it." He stated.

He handed the scope to me, I clambered up level with him, rather conscious of how exposed we were, but darkness was our friend for the time being. I put the scope to my eye. The scope gave you a very bright light green image in the darkness, revealing our Second Battalion moving very slowly in their heavily loaded columns towards their start lines. I didn't envy them. This was their second battle. Goose Green by the sounds of things had really set the tone for this land campaign. I felt a pang of guilt, since Wireless Ridge was meant to be one of our objectives. The enemy strength and with it their resistance on Longdon really put us in the hurt locker, resulting in one hell of a body count on both sides.

The distant thunder of our guns began, their projectiles streaked overhead on route to their mark. The shells then began to burst above Wireless Ridge, bathing the whole feature in brilliant light. Davo's scope was now rendered useless since the flares spoilt the image it provided. As the flares drifted across the ridge, no movement could be seen amongst the rock spines that lined the feature. The enemy were good at not showing their cards too early. As the flares faded out, fresh flares burst above, keeping the light constant. The silent approach option was not what was on the cards by the looks of things. Those fuckers who withdrew from our assault last night where about to get another helping of carnage, chaos and mayhem on their new position.

Off to the north of the ridge, all hell was unleashed. A huge volume of red tracer came screaming in, smashing their recorded targets. Some of the enemy scampered like ants from their untenable positions, which were getting obliterated by this sheer weight of fire. As they fell back to rear positions, huge explosions smashed along the feature shredding anyone caught in the open. This was the Royal Navy's contribution to the attack. Milan missiles now joined in with the killing, smashing bunkers, causing the roofs to cave in and crush those not brave enough to fall back through the naval gunfire. We had one hell of a ringside seat, the flares remained constant throughout the battle, and Ford Coppola couldn't create anything like this for Hollywood.

Coming into the flare footprint now was the lead companies of the Second Battalion. Advancing very spaced out. As they drew near the forward positions they would then scamper about in pairs and so on, dealing with the bunkers in turn. The thuds of their grenades were drowned out by the deafening soundtrack of their fire support. As they got themselves sorted out round the bunkers, shells would smash all over their location, causing them to scatter like ants into whatever cover was available. The Argentinians were not going quietly. Second Battalion would pay for any real estate they captured, that was very evident from our own experiences on Longdon. Once the counter bombardment ceased, they would emerge from whatever cover they managed to find and then continue pushing forward.

Movement behind us broke our gaze as Leighton and Zane scrambled up to us covered in blankets and allsorts.

"Here you go guys, they don't smell too great, but they will do the job."

Zane handed me a blanket, which was damp to the touch and smelt absolutely vile, a mixture of mouldy cheese and body odour. The cold had really settled in now, and the snowflakes were getting bigger and were settling on the rocks around us. I wrapped the blanket around me, which help keep the wind off me if anything, the smell I would just have to put up with. We were now all wrapped up with smelly blankets and sleeping bags, and we looked a right state. Who would think we were a professional army? More like conscripts on the retreat from Moscow. We then went back to watching the battle raging before us. As the Second Battalion took ground, the Argentines would shell their lost positions, which made life difficult and progress slow. In the flare light, you could just make out, small groups of enemy troops moving back off Wireless Ridge and trying to make their way back to Moody Brook barracks which stood in the darkness, just outside the flare footprint. Our Artillery got wise to this, as shells splashed amongst the withdrawing enemy. The artillery was wreaking havoc amongst the enemy, since shells would land amongst them; they would all dive to the ground, but every time this happened, less and less were getting back up. Some did manage to get out of the glare of our flares, but not many.

What happened then was one of the strangest things I'd ever seen. There was a large puff of smoke amongst the small houses on the outskirts of Stanley itself, and a white flash of light streaked off across Wireless Ridge and out to sea at an amazing rate of knots. Whatever it was, and whether it was meant to be for our guys on the Ridge, fuck knows! Strange.

More and more of the enemy were now falling back off Wireless Ridge and trying to make their escape through our artillery. It made for grim watching. It just shredded those caught in the open. Tracer from Second Battalion began to cut them down as well, since the reverse slope positions were now in their hands. Few flares were now in the air and our grandstand view of the attack was reducing by the minute. The attack had lasted a good few hours, but to me it seemed it had only started about an hour ago. The flare light faded. The show as far as we were concerned was over.

Second Battalion were now taking care of their grim business in the dark. I pitied those Argentines foolish enough to still be holding out, it would not end well for them. We turned in towards each other, and let out a small nervous chuckle at our own predicament. Cold, dirty, exhausted. There was light off to our right, the Battle for Tumbledown was still in full swing. Flares drifted above its peak, machine guns chattered, tracer flicking skywards, shells smashing into the summit. I didn't know much about the Scots Guards, but I felt sorry for those fighting for their lives trying to keep a Battalion of cold, tired Scotsmen from the chance of a bed and a bath in Stanley.

"Right that's it", Davo piped up, "I'm chinned; let's get some kip, more adventures tomorrow."

Murmurs in agreement from the rest of us. We tucked ourselves into whatever crags in the alleys walls there were. I was now glad of my new duvet jacket, and I understood why I'd been given just a blanket. Most of the lads only had their issued quilted suits; they were just not good enough in this weather, which was clear to see. My own quilted trousers were shredded in my barrel bag, so I therefore had to suffer with cold legs for the night. My feet were frozen, but there was not much I could do about it until daylight at least. Little sleep was to be had, despite how shattered I was. It was just too damn cold. I would drift off, and wake up a few seconds later shivering my tits off. The soundtrack of Tumbledown was still full force across the valley. The wind sweeping up the alley chilled us all to the bone. What also played on my shattered mind was what would be happening tomorrow? Planning for street fighting? I had images of Arnhem and Stalingrad in my head, when the front line couldn't be marked on a map, but measured in who occupied which room and which floor. Street fighting was savage at best; you could be right on top of your enemy to the point where your weapons were just not effective in such a confined space such as a bedroom or basement. Hand to hand fighting would normally be what was needed to subdue an enemy in them tight spots, literally beating each other to death with whatever was to hand, furniture, fists, knifes found in kitchen drawers, you name it. Artillery would be no good to us once we broke into the town, since our observers could not ensure that friendly forces would not be caught in their own barrages. What if the Argentines make a last stand in the sewers of Stanley? Many a tale of Stalingrad told you of grim skirmishes in the pitch black shit-smeared tunnels under a cold shattered city.

What about Snipers? A smashed up town is ideal cover for the defender, a living nightmare for the attacker. I'm confident in the ability of our Snipers, but being a machine gunner, I'm certainly on the menu for enemy sharpshooters. Many previous conflicts in cities generate stories of relaxing troops getting their head shattered by the snipers bullet. Just the one shot, which breeds panic amongst his comrades, who will not be able to relax anywhere in that area. What have you got yourself into Archie boy?

Tumbledown had now ceased to be background noise for the night. I only hoped it ended in our favour. It sounded pretty intense at some points through the night as I shivered under my stinking blanket trying to rest. I pulled the blanket from my face and peered down the alley to where what was left of our company was trying to do the same. Some stood in small groups, smoking and chatting. Some had even got their hexi burners out and had started cooking. Dawn was on its way as daylight began to make an appearance off to the east. I looked over to my right and caught Jamie starting to fidget under his captured sleeping bag. Keeping his head covered, he cocked his right leg in the air and let off a really squeaky fart that echoed down the alley, causing the lads huddled around a burner to look up at us and begin to chuckle. Jamie then sat bolt upright.

"I think someone has taken a shit in my mouth."

Charming. To be fair, he had a point; it had been a while since any of us had brushed our teeth.

"What time is it?"

"Daytime". I couldn't be arsed to look at my watch.

"Hey" he grinned, "I do the jokes, and you do the cooking."

With the blanket draped over my shoulders, I went about getting breakfast on the go. Most of the company were up and moving by this point, all with the same thing in mind. I stood up, and let out an almighty stretch. I stood at the top of the alley looking out towards Wireless Ridge and Stanley. The street lights were slowly going out as daylight became established. I could see clearly the Second Battalion milling about on their positions. Apart from the wind, all was quiet. Peering down, at the base of the bowl, I could see what I could only guess was C Company beginning to move off in the direction of Wireless. They marched in two columns, which began to climb over the saddle that separated Longdon from the Wireless feature. Further off to the right, some distance away was the shattered remains of Moody Brook Barracks, their objective. I went back to tend to breakfast which I had neglected and by the looks of things, Jamie had taken up the role of chef.

As we sat there and ate, there was commotion at the bottom of the alley. Justin and Dale were moving from group to group, and as they moved on, the groups were hugging and back slapping each other. Davo had woken and sat up scratching his head, and I could see his eyes narrow to focus on what the hell was going on. Justin and Dale reached us.

"The Argentines have called for a ceasefire" Justin's face was all smiles, "Second Battalion are moving through Moody Brook now and pushing up to the racecourse, make safe your weapons. Enjoy your breakfast."

With that they turned and made their way back down, Dale giving me a wink as they left.

Numb was an understatement. Davo put his face in his hands, his shoulders bouncing as he began to sob. No more killing. I could see Jamie's eyes had glazed over, and tears began to roll down his face as he gave me a beaming smile. We didn't speak for a while; we just sat there, in our own thoughts, tears rolling down our filthy faces. No more killing. No one needed to die today, no one.

13

We made our weapons safe. Still loaded, but in order to fire them, you had to cock a round into the breach before they would work, it all felt like the end of an exercise. I unloaded the gimpy completely and ensured the working parts of the gun were forward, then placed the belt back on. We packed away our kit and waited for Dale to call us down into the RAP, hopefully for the last time. We just sat there, grinning at each other. No gunfire, no shelling, no screaming, no dying, it felt fucking wonderful. The word came and we all clambered to our feet and shuffled down out of this horrible world of rock and shit. We skirted right back around towards the RAP, everyone in single file, purely out of habit, both hands on our weapons, since it could all go wrong with the Second Battalion hard on the heels of those Argentines legging it back into Stanley.

The RAP looked a lot different this morning, our dead and wounded had been back loaded, probably to Teal, the enemy dead were nowhere to be seen, either buried or back loaded also. The prisoners were being marched back to Estancia no doubt. Sadness hit me square in the face at this point, all those guys, theirs and ours that had been killed or wounded so close to the end, so sad. Once at the RAP, we noticed everyone was just milling about out in the open, not seeking shelter amongst the boulders and rocks through fear of shelling. Some of those gathered had removed their helmets, clipping them onto their belt kit. Justin and Dale walked amongst us wearing their maroon berets and shaking hands with us all. This felt rather bizarre, it was only a couple of days ago they were shaking our hands prior to the attack. Everyone began putting their berets on. I fished mine out of my smock inside pocket. It was in abit of a state, damp from my own sweat, covered in bits of fluff and the kind of random crap that gathers in ones pockets after a while. I gave it a good shake and picked the worse of the fluff and crap off it and placed it onto my head. There is a certain way the British soldier wears their beret, if they wear it as the regulations say, you look like Benny Hill, and so you have to push your luck abit with regards to style. In our Battalion, we would have the bottom tip of our cap badge between the left eye and ear, so you didn't look like a right Wally when it came to being in the public eye. Beret firmly on my head, I clipped my helmet to the back of my webbing.

"Prepare to move," Dale called out to us.

I didn't want to march into town with the duvet jacket on, so I scrambled out of my gear, removed it, place my fighting gear back on, and Jamie stuffed the jacket through the yolk straps between my back and the top of my pouches. I'd lost track of my barrel bag, and there was not much I could do about it now. Our company began to shuffle forward in two columns towards Wireless Ridge, just as we did marching from San Carlos. A Company had already moved off from their position, and were making their way to Moody Brook. Gimpy over my right shoulder, I followed the column over the saddle that separated Wireless from Longdon. In the distance, near the water's edge I could see columns of troops marching along. There was talk amongst the column of a possible minefield, but this didn't slow us down in the slightest. We were heading in the direction of Moody Brook Barracks which was on the western edge of the bay that Port Stanley sits on. The barracks was the home of a small Commando garrison when the Argentines invaded. It was destroyed in the initial invasion; luckily the Commandos had abandoned it sometime the day before.

We encountered a number of enemy dead on our way towards the barracks. Shredded by our artillery as they fled towards Stanley. We gave them a token glance then moved on, we'd seen enough of death, we just wanted to get this over with and go home. As we drew alongside the barracks, it was just a burnt out wreck of a site. Some of our lads, not too sure which company, were dealing with a couple of prisoners who must have sheltered there after the onslaught of the night before. They finished searching them, gave them a cigarette, and walked with them onto the tarmac road that connected the barracks to the town. Truly remarkable, no rough treatment, both sides walking down the road, smoking cigarettes, relieved it was over. No one had to die today. As I made my way onto the tarmac, it felt like a gift from the gods. Up until now, it was just cold rain soaked peat or tussock grass beating up my feet, but now we had tarmac, it felt great. The local council had its work cut out, the road was covered in all sorts of crap, mud, blood, ammunition, weapons, bloody bandages, spent bullet casings, all the clutter that comes with battle. It was all over the shop; we just stepped over it and moved on. We encountered more enemy dead on the road; someone had taken the time to cover them up with some corrugated sheeting, their boots poking out of one end, such a shame.

We were then told to hold up. We just all bunched up and pushed over to the right side of the road, and sat down. Word came down the line that we were to give the Argentines some breathing space as they left the town and gathered on the airfield further to the east. Some would argue this was unwise, to give an enemy such room to move, but orders were orders. As we sat there a steady stream of what could only be our Second Battalion were marching past on their way into town. So why had we been told to stay put? I stood up and looked down the road into town. It quickly dawned on me that Stanley was in bad shape, a couple of buildings were on fire, all sorts of gear strewn all over the road, it no longer gave you the feel of an oasis when we were on Longdon, probably nothing more than a ransacked fishing town.

Word came down the line for us to move; everyone got to their feet, and adjusted their loads. We then shuffled off down the road towards town, and very soon we were veering off to the right onto the racecourse. Hardly Kempton Park, the Argentines had trashed it. The gun line was established there, loads of artillery pieces pointing towards the mountains, with crude earthworks and turfs piled up around them in an attempt to conceal them and protect their crews. Empty shell cases were strewn all over the place, crates of ammunition were piled up behind the guns, open to the elements. I'm sure members of the Royal Artillery upon seeing this shambles of a gun line would have a heart attack at such disarray. Trenches next to their positions, which I'm assuming for the gun crews were filled to the brim with water, and the tents alongside, were just rain soaked canvas hovels. Did they sleep in the houses? Or just slum it the best they could out in the open? We made our way through the gun line towards the first cluster of bungalows. Small trampled hedgerows separated the gun line and the town, and it was here we were told to go firm. It started to rain, and some of the guys got their ponchos out and pitched them up along whatever fence lines were available. Others got brews on the go, cigarettes were smoked, and jokes were cracked, usual shit. A few of the lads ventured forward towards the bungalows and peered through the windows. They then turned around, shrugged their shoulders and made their way back to us pitching up camp. Word was soon passed around not to break into any of the houses, due to possible booby traps, and we had to wait for engineers to clear them. Moans and groans swept through us like wildfire, with certain anonymous voices commenting on officers merely playing for time whilst they looked for the best beds and baths. It did cross my mind, don't get me wrong, but to be honest, as long as we eventually got out of the weather, I didn't give a monkeys where I slept. I'd lost track of Jamie and I went in search of him, when I found him he was under a poncho, Hot Chocolate ready to go and a cheeky grin on his face.

"Took your time, I got bored of waiting."

I scrambled out of my fighting gear and slipped the duvet jacket over my smock, and slid underneath to join him. We had to stay put for most of the day, as engineers ensured the bungalows we wanted to occupy were cleared of booby traps and the like. We mainly just stood around waiting for this to be complete. Out on the road, columns of Commandos with their heavy packs had made their way out of the mountains and were trudging into Stanley. They were all full of smiles, and we would exchange professional nods to each other. There was nothing more than professional rivalry between us and them, only the minority of clowns would make out it to be any deeper than that. The Commandos had their fair share of misery on this fucking island, and to top it off, theyd slogged it out with bergens. Our bergens had yet to be brought forward from Estancia, but if we were indoors tonight, it shouldn't be too much of a discomfort.

Word come round that the buildings were clear and we could now occupy them. The owners were staying with friends further into town in order to make room for their liberators, bloody nice of them. Dale rallied the company and gave us a heads up.

"Right lads, I will show you to your accommodation, a Platoon at a time, but I must warn you now, they are trashed, the Argentines have shit and pissed everywhere, and it looks like they've burgled the place as well."

For fuck sake, what was their thing with shitting everywhere?

"4 Platoon, get your gear and follow me." Dale ordered.

As they were led off to their bungalows, Davo ordered 5 Platoon to gear up and get ready. We could hear 4 Platoon cursing out loud at the state of their dwellings, which made the rest of the company chuckle, don't know why we were so smug, we had yet to see ours.

"5 Platoon." Dale bellowed.

We made our way over, and he led us through the first row of buildings to ours, which from the outside didn't look too bad. The owners must have had small children, since there was a swing and slide, plus random childrens toys strewn about the garden. We set foot inside and the stench of shit and piss hit us square in the face. It was all over the floor, even on the kitchen units, why would you do this? It's just not civilized, war or not. Davo had seen enough.

"Right, everyone get outside, drop your gear off, we need to blitz it room by room."

We all got outside and stripped off all our gear, down to just shirts, preparing to do some serious housework. Davo spammed Jamie and I with collecting up all the shit that was literally everywhere, being the newest Private soldiers in the Platoon, this was our chore. Leighton and Zane grinned at us menacingly under their bushy gringo tashes, since it clearly wasn't going to be them on poo picking duty. Their faces dropped when Davo spammed them with clearing all the shit smeared furniture out of the bungalow and putting it in the garden. They glared at us, but we avoided their hard stares and found hunting for turds very interesting. Davo put others to task clearing out the remainder of the rubbish strewn all over the place, plus sweeping and mopping etc. How bizarre was this whole experience? This time yesterday, we were getting shelled on a mountainside, and today, we are sweeping and mopping out a bungalow, Hollywood gets war films wrong every time. The whole effort took the better part of a couple of hours, the bungalow was clear, but almost bare since alot of the furniture was not fit for use, and stacked up in the garden. This worked in our favour; we had more floor space to get everyone in and settled. The whole place now reeked with bleach, which burned the nostrils, but we were enjoying luxury. A kitchen which allowed us to eat in a human fashion. A toilet and bathroom to get ourselves clean. Clean!

There was a knock at the front door, which felt weird, and in strolled Dale with Justin doing the rounds.

"Blimey fellas", Dale chuckled "very plush."

We were rather proud of our efforts. They had a sneaky nose about our place, nodding in approval of our efforts. We knew what was coming next; they were just hedging their bets on which Platoon to live with.

"Got any room for us?" Justin got to the point.

Davo looked at the floor, shaking his head, chuckling.

"Yes Sir, let me do a bit of a re shuffle, and we will get you in." Davo would now be known to the Platoon as Basil.

As they left to carry on their inspections, Dale let us know the bergens were on their way in by Chinook onto the racecourse. We bundled out with just our weapons, and as we made our way through the gardens, you could hear the drumming thud of its rotor blades getting louder. We gathered on the edge of the racecourse as the huge heavily loaded beast hovered about a hundred metres away. Beneath it was a huge cargo net full to capacity with bergens and kit bags. Just as it made contact with the ground, whatever was used to connect it to the helicopter came loose, and the huge bundle thudded on the turf. The Chinook remained in the hover and turned to the left, showing us its tailgate and then landed just behind the bundle. Amid the din of rotors and engines, not to mention the monstrous draft that almost pushed you over if you were not braced for it, the tail gate lowered to expose two figures, one of which was the loadmaster. He got the ramp as he wanted it and then gave us the thumbs up. Dale returned the gesture, and with a wave of his right arm led us forward towards the bundle and the aircraft. The draft from the rotors intensified as we walked closer; in a half crouch kind of waddle. As we got to the bundle, Dale turned on us and placed his hand on the left shoulder of a number of us, including me, pointing at the remainder to deal with the bergens, he waved us on towards the Chinook.

The noise was a deafening whine as the engines continued to run. As we got closer, the surface water of the racecourse stung our faces as we made our way to the tailgate. This was short lived since we were now getting the benefits of being behind the aircraft. The engines dried us off almost instantly, and for a short while was a wonderful feeling. I quickly recognised the second person on the tailgate; it was Phil, our Company Quartermaster Sergeant. I hadn't seen him since San Carlos; he shook hands with Dale who then turned to me waving me onto the ramp. Phil didn't waste any time or fuel talking to me, he just handed me more bergens, kitbags, ammo, rations, jerry cans of water, plus other random crap. I merely spun round and handed them to the guy behind me, who happened to be Dale. He had arranged a human chain just to quickly get all the gear off the aircraft as quickly as possible. In this fashion, we'd quickly emptied the aircraft. As we were waved of the ramp, Phil was using a torch to check the inside of the aircraft just in case we left anything behind. Happy we had not missed anything he shook hands with the loadmaster, and joined us as we crouched down over our kit. The ramp went up and then the whole pitch of the engine noise increased as this huge machine began to climb into the air once again, its rotor down draft pressing us hard into the kit we had just unloaded. The din began to subside, and the Chinook was on its way back into the mountains for its next task.

For the next hour or so it was all hands to the pump getting our Company stores over to the bungalows. 4 Platoon had taken alot of casualties so therefore had the most room in which to get Phil and our stores under cover, out of the elements. Once all the humping and dumping was complete, we shouldered our bergens and made our way back to our little palace. The bungalow was now cluttered with peoples kit getting pulled from bergens as we got ourselves comfortable. Davo has given Company Headquarters the master bedroom which made space in the living room abit tighter, but we managed. I unrolled my sleeping bag, and sat on it getting totally stripped off. I then stood up and whipped on a clean pair of boxer shorts, but gave my body abit of a once over. Back at home, it could be safely said, I was somewhat tubbier than the majority of our Platoon, not unfit, just not very toned. My ribcage was very prominent now, all my excess weight burnt off during our series of marches and living on rations. My legs we well defined, since they had received a big workout tabbing everywhere. I had sores on my hips and the base of my back from where my webbing had rubbed. My feet didn't look too clever, not in pain or anything; they'd just not seen the light of day for some time. Pretty much everyone in the living room had the same idea as me, for a male civilian, being crammed into a room with a load of semi naked men could cause some discomfort, but soldiers are well past giving a fuck, considering what we had all been through in the last couple of weeks. Once I was content I wasn't going to keel over and die anytime soon, I treated myself to a fresh pair of socks and a clean shirt, and got dressed again, my trainers were on for the time being.

For a while, I just lay on my sleeping bag as the lads got themselves sorted, and after a time the chaos that had dominated the room subsided, ending with rather content men lying on their bags, either smoking, picking their noses, or having a scratch. The room now had the aroma of toothpaste, foot powder, cigarette smoke, farts, and feet, the usual odour of a barrack block. Jamie, who was pitched up to my right was out for the count, open mouthed like he was trying to catch flies, snoring his head off. I sat up and looked around my immediate area for something to throw at him, but to no avail. Someone had AC/DC beating out a track on a tape recorder in one of the bedrooms, which got my foot tapping and the constant beating of drums was making me doze off. What could only have been a few minutes had actually been an hour or so. I felt a nudge, I opened one eye and Jamie was sat up looking at Justin and Dale stood in the centre of the room. As I sat up, I noticed the whole room was crammed with everyone from the Company, something was afoot.

"Gentlemen" Justin paused.

He had our attention.

"The Argentine forces have formally surrendered."

Tear filled eyes and beaming smiles filled the room in an instant.

"General Moore took the surrender about ten minutes ago; the Argentine General Menendez has signed a document stating that Argentina will cease all operations on both East and West Falkland. It's over. Congratulations and very well done."

Fantastic. No one else had to die.

We could all see Justin starting to well up, and when he grabbed Dale in a big bear hug, we all cheered as this let the tension out of the room. We all stood up shaking hands with each other; tears rolling down all our faces, the moment was just too nice an occasion to really give a toss about the macho image we liked to portray. This war was over, and this meant we could go home soon, see our parents, our children, our wives and girlfriends. Fucking brilliant. Once all the hugging and back slapping had run its course, Dale wiped the tears from his eyes and called for order. We then quietened down.

"Right lads, we've now got a rather pissed off defeated army sat out at the airport, who still have their weapons and ammo with them. The Commandos have been tasked with disarming them in the morning, and then they will be put to task with clearing up this town, since they made the bloody mess."

Some tittering could be heard with nods of agreement.

"Our Company has been tasked with clearing up the racecourse, using prisoners to do the donkey work. You are there to guard them, not talk about the football, and just make sure they behave and do the clear up, understood?"

We all nodded, I'd forgotten about the football.

"Right then," he continued, "get some rest, I want at least two people awake at any one time, so we can respond to any sudden dramas in the night. Have a fag and a brew by the front door, whatever, just be awake. Anyone fucks this up, their entire Platoon will move out onto the racecourse, is that clear?"

A chorus of "yes Sir" was heard across the room, no one wanted to sleep outside anymore. With that, the other Platoons departed and we got ourselves settled. No one appeared to be in a rush to get some sleep, many still high on the surrender news, me included. Jamie and I went into the kitchen to see if the kettle worked, it did, bonus. The plumbing was abit ropey and the water was just a trickle out of the taps, so we used what water we had in our webbing. With brews in hand we made our way to the front door. Davo, Leighton and Zane were on the porch. Davo had his rifle across his knees, giving it a clean whilst the other two hoods were trying to tune in a little radio they had found, probably trying to get the football. These two goons frowned more and more as they tried to get a signal, and their gringo tashes made them look all the more sinister.

"You okay guys?" Davo piped up once he realised we were there.

"Yeah, not bad at all." Jamie answered. "Just glad it's over."

Davo grinned and nodded, and focused on the rifle in his lap.

"You lads did well up there." He pointed off into the distance, Wireless Ridge was in plain view and in the fading light, and you could just make out the summit of Longdon peering over the top. It looked a million miles away. He continued.

"All we need to do now is get this town back into shape, and get the hell out of here."

As he finished speaking, the gruesome twosome dropped the radio on the floor, Leighton stamped on it and stormed inside, whilst Zane remained, putting a cigarette between his lips, as he lit it, he mumbled.

"Fucking thing"

Davo looked up at him as he blew his first plume of smoke into the air, then at me before looking back to his weapon, shoulders bouncing as he stifled a chuckle. Zane was a horrible looking bastard, you would not want him playing Father Christmas at your kids' party, put it that way, but up on Longdon he was solid as a rock. When Dale pushed me back up to join the Platoon after I had fallen in that trench, Zane had got to grips with me and gave me an update of what was going on and where, which goes to show that Private soldiers can read the battle as it unfolds around them. Me personally, I wouldn't have received man of the match with regards to the battle, since for the majority of the assault, I was just a fat sweaty mess, and not entirely sure of what was going on. Zane would get my vote.

Cheering could be heard further into town, as news of the surrender had spread. As happy as I was that this whole terrible episode would nearly be over for us, I couldn't help but feel sadness for those who were not here to share in the celebrations. I didn't envy the Argentines either, as they made their way to the airport and awaited processing tomorrow. I didn't know if they had enough shelter tonight, but at least they were alive to complain about such conditions. Reflecting on some of the enemy dead we encountered on Longdon really hit home how brutally them guys met their deaths. Our boys had destroyed those positions and them men with extreme violence. Bodies and bunkers riddled with bullet holes, half naked men caught clambering out of tents and sleeping bags splintered by grenades and bayonets as our guys rolled through their positions. Brave defenders crushed by their own bunkers as anti tank missiles collapsed them. Terrified conscripts put to the bayonet in the horrific night fighting amongst the rocks. A truly grim experience for both sides.

As I made my way back into the bungalow, most of the lads had now settled down for the night, chatting quietly amongst themselves. Jamie was already back in his bag, and having a good old pick of his nose before turning in for the night. I stripped down to just my boxer shorts and clambered in. It felt so nice not to have to wear all of your clothing, the sleeping bag felt huge on me, due to the fact I was just in my boxers. I didn't smell too great, but that could all be dealt with tomorrow. AC/DC had called it a night by this point as well since its owner had probably either turned in or been told to turn it off. No doubt in the night I would be woken for a stint keeping watch at the front door, but I would just deal with that when I got a shove.

14

I felt a shove, and I felt it was my turn to stand watch. As I pulled the sleeping bag from my drool smeared face, I could see it was early dawn. People were dressed and milling around with cups of tea and cigarettes on the go. I leaned over to Jamie, who was doing his boot laces up.

"Good morning handsome, want a brew?"

I sat up, fearful of a swift reprisal for missing my turn on watch. None came.

"Why did no one wake me?" I mumbled.

"Fuck knows, no one woke me either, I heard some of the lads chatting and smoking by the door all night, maybe they couldn't sleep."

I clambered out of the bag and sat on it cross legged just trying to tune in. Some of the Platoon were still sound asleep, which made me feel more relaxed. Dale walked in through the front door fully dressed and called for everyone's attention. Those asleep were nudged awake.

"Guys, the Commandos have started processing the prisoners. Don't expect to see any with us for a few hours. Take this time to get your admin sorted. I want to see clean shaven faces, plus polish on boots. The media are going to be around here soon like flies around a turd, so don't show yourselves up. If they ask you about Longdon, refer them to me or the O.C for the clean, edited version, understood?"

We all nodded.

"Engineers and some Artillery punters are gonna be here soon, to ensure the gun line can be moved, so don't go fucking about with their Artillery, some may be booby trapped or still loaded from the other night."

With that, he made his way into the master bedroom. I perched up on my knees at the end of my bag and began to rifle through my bergen. I rubbed my hand over my face, and I could no longer get away with not shaving, it had been a few days since my last flirt with a razor. My boxers and socks were fresh from yesterday, so I got dressed and with my shaving kit, made my way outside. Some of the lads were stripped to the waist around a saucepan of hot water on top of an oil drum, scraping hair and old cam cream off their faces for the first time in days. The transformation I watched as they shaved was amazing, changing from rough, grizzled combat veterans, back to young fresh faced lads in a few strokes of a razor. I looked twelve most of the time, and at the moment I just looked like a twelve year old with too much bum fluff, so the shaving effect wouldn't be too much of a change. Once a gap presented itself for me to squeeze into, I got on with my ablutions. Once all sorted and teeth brushed, I got fully dressed and awaited our workforce of Argentine prisoners.

The platoon was all shaved and polished by the time our workforce had arrived. A small group of Commandos had marched them in some kind of military order up to our meeting point. Dale exchanged a few words with their escorts who then left them under our charge for the remainder of the day. Dale had arranged for some of our guys to get a couple of captured trucks up to the racecourse in order to tow the guns out on to the beach, so they were out of the way. Dale then assigned groups of prisoners to the platoons for the day's task. 4 Platoon would move all the live ammunition to the beach for collection by the Royal Engineers. They had a full day's work ahead of them, because there was fuck loads of it. Our Platoon would get the guns hitched up to the trucks and get them off the racecourse. Once done, we would then help 6 Platoon clear all the remaining crap from the race course that didn't belong there. It was going to be a long cold day.

The original plan for 4 Platoon soon went to rat shit, due to the fact that there was far too much for 4 Platoon to shift on their own. There was tons of the stuff, most of it artillery shells. I had never seen such vast quantities of ammo in one place. It made the ammo stacked up at San Carlos on the first day look poxy in comparison. Our gunners probably dreamed of having such vast amounts available to them, certainly during this campaign. If they had really gone to town on us as we hunkered down on Longdon, they could have really given us a good hiding. Bearing in mind the quality of the gun crews and their observers, Conscript or Regular? I would like to think that Regular gunners would have given us a real run for our money, and maybe kept a tidier gun line. The whole company, prisoners included, got to grips with the ammo, just to get it cleared. It took hours. Every time we moved to a new gun position, we would have to wait for the Engineers to ensure it was safe to start clearing it. It was late afternoon by the time the majority of the ammo was shifted over to the beach. We then left 4 Platoon to finish off the last couple of positions, while us and 6 Platoon went back to our original tasks.

Our job was pretty straight forward, hitch the guns up and drag them over to the beach. The trucks all had towing hooks, but we didn't have the means to connect them to the guns. Dale came over with some ratchet straps he must have scrounged from somewhere and dropped them at our prisoner's feet.

"Don't worry about the lawn; just get the things dragged out of here."

With that, we literally strapped the trailing legs of the gun to the back of the truck, and our driver have it plenty of gas, and dragged it off the racecourse, ploughing as it went. Well, it couldn't make this bloody position any more worst, the Argentines had long past caring about the lawn. We were in the process of connecting up the second gun, when we heard some old fella in flat cap and Barbour jacket, come over ranting and raving about what we had done to his precious furlong. He demanding to speak to those in command, and we pointed him in the direction of Dale, who was stood near the bungalows, having a brew with the O.C. He stormed away in their direction, leaving us to continue ploughing the guns over to the beach. Fuck knows what he said to them, neither Justin nor Dale rushed over to reprimand us. Ungrateful arsehole.

With the ammo and guns shifted, all we had left to do was help 6 Platoon clear the remainder of random crap scattered all over the shop. Dale got bored with the whole enterprise by early evening, and told us it could wait till the morning. The Commando escorts for our prisoners were already waiting on the road for them. As our prisoners made their way over to the road, some had the cheek to ask some of us for cigarettes. What harm could it do? Zane surprised me the most and gave them a whole packet and a thumbs up. They waved goodbye to us and got into some kind of order on the road and wandered off with their escorts back to the airport. They weren't a bad bunch to be fair, they did as they were told without complaint, and chatted away in Spanish, the occasional chuckle and a high five here and there. To be honest, if they were happy, probably less chance of a revolt. They just wanted to go home, me too. During the course of the day, shifting that ammo with the gimpy slung across my back was a royal pain in the arse, but Dale insisted we remained armed. The racecourse was two thirds clear, just the remaining shite to clear in the morning. We wandered back to our bungalows for a well deserved brew and something to eat.

Back at the bungalow, the usual admin chaos ensued. Talk of a church service the following afternoon was doing the rounds, which wasn't a problem, since it wouldn't be long before we got the job on the racecourse finished. There was what appeared to be media loitering between the bungalows, snapping away with their cameras, and trying to strike up conversation with whoever was outside having a fag. I played it safe and stayed in the bungalow; I would only drop myself in the shit for expressing an opinion that would make headline news. Better for them to interview Officers, who could dazzle them with long complicated words they learned at University and Sandhurst. Archie from Portsmouth, with his cat-sat–on-the-mat schooling and vocabulary would not make for good reading at the best of times, so I kept out of their way.

In the kitchen there was commotion and the rattling of pots and pans. I peered around the door, and I could see Leighton and Zane, with their sleeves rolled up, getting stuck into some serious cooking. On the counter next to them was a large cardboard box of rations, with gold tins of various grub scattered all over the place. The pot they were stirring and heating was massive as they continued to pour random sludge from various tins into it. I ducked back out of sight in case they caught me and put me on washing up duty. I went back over to where my sleeping bag was and unslung the gun and parked my arse. Jamie was oblivious to my arrival, as he was routing through his bergen for something. I gave him a nudge, which made him jump.

"What is Pinky and Perky up to in the kitchen?"

"I think they are doing an "all in" for the Platoon" he replied.

An "all in" is a soldiers term for mass feeding. Instead of us all trying to cook our individual meals all over the bungalow garden, it makes sense to exploit the kitchen facilities at hand, and feed us all at once. Nice idea. We couldn't use the hexi burners indoors because the fumes from the tablets are poisonous in the right quantities. Before long, Zane peered around the door, announcing dinner was ready. The usual jibes about food poisoning echoed around the room, but we all lined up for our share. I wasn't going to complain, I couldn't be arsed to go out into the cold and cook my own anyway. The loitering media would only ruin my appetite. As I arrived at the front of the queue, they scooped my helping into my mess tin, and it was then they broadsided me with the pan washing after dinner. Bastards. They told me to bring my girlfriend to dry up, indicating Jamie. I chuckled, which caught Jamie's attention. It quickly dawned on him what they were saying. He quickly had an answer for them.

"I will have you know gentlemen, that I pitch, and my fair lady here catches."

The gruesome twosome just rolled their eyes, and reminded us we were on washing up detail after scoff, and less of the lip.

The food wasn't at all bad. It was a stew of sorts, just a random selection of meat, veg and a shit load of gravy thrown in, with a job lot of hard tack biscuits thrown in to thicken it up. It was hot, it was simple, and it filled the hole. Davo asked out loud what was for pudding. Leighton informed him that it was whatever we could find for ourselves in the box. You just can't beat this type of customer service. I enjoyed the stew that much; I went up for another helping, which started a slow trickle of diners to do the same. It wasn't long before the large pot was as good as bare and I could commence with the washing up. There wasn't any washing up liquid, but I found a semi clean rag under the sink, and just made sure the water was hot enough to do the job. Jamie wandered in and sat on the counter next to the sink.

"You'd think your shit job stint would have died with Danny wouldn't you."

It didn't get the giggle he was after, I didn't find it funny. I just looked into the water, Danny leant against the bunker, face smashed in by tracer, arm almost ripped off, his torso riddled with machine gun fire. I'm sure I'm not the only soldier that has ever thought about their demise in the heat of battle, guns blazing, with an awesome soundtrack as your last action destroys the enemy. I watched Danny die the other night, it wasn't in a blaze of glory, he was pulverized beyond recognition in a fraction of a second by a machine gunner who was mutually supporting the bunker Danny had just assaulted. Well sited, very deadly, nothing more. It is very cliché to think that it should be Danny stood over you when you are badly wounded, because that's the way it works on exercise. It didn't go that way at all the other night, before we knew it, we had a Lance Corporal as the Platoon Commander, with whatever Private soldiers who had the balls to step up and take command of the chaos in the cold darkness. It's true what they say; you are just one bullet away from being in charge. I felt a hand on my shoulder which snapped me out of it.

"Sorry mate," Jamie grinned, "bad timing."

I smiled, it wasn't his fault, it's just business. With that, I set about scrubbing the pan. Without washing up liquid, I wasn't really getting anywhere. Jamie routed through a few drawers and found a tea towel, so we just wiped the pan dry and in the process, removed the remains of the stew, done. We went back into the living room, to find the lads just lying about, chatting quietly and smoking. Considering the conflict was as good as over, it felt more of an anti-climax. I had the impression we could not go home until Stanley was back in some sort of order. I got undressed and climbed into my bag, and just pondered in my thoughts. I just wanted to go home.

Morning came with no fanfare, just the usual routine of ablutions and feeding. Once shaved, dressed and fed, I made my way outside just to get out of the way, since there wasn't much room in there with everyone trying to do the same thing. We had another problem on our hands now. I'm not sure if it was Zane and Leighton's cooking, but a few of the lads in the night had to make a dash to the toilet. The plumbing couldn't cope with the volume of customers, so some had to just dash out into the cold night, in just underwear and shit in the bushes at the end of the garden. Some didn't make it. Toilet roll was abit of a scarce commodity in Port Stanley at this time, and if all the troops crammed into it suffered with the shits, things could get rather grim around here, very quickly. I wasn't feeling the effects as of yet, but Jamie admitted feeling rather ropey. He realised this when he went to conduct his morning fart, when he all of a sudden lost confidence in the outcome, and had to dash away to avoid a disaster. Dale and Justin returned from their morning meeting with the C.O and gave us the news that our church service was postponed twenty four hours since it became apparent that the entire Battalion wasn't faring any better. But the clearance of the racecourse would continue. Our group of prisoners arrived once again, and we got to work clearing up what was left around the gun positions. Our prisoners found it a source of entertainment when their armed guards would have to scamper over to the hedges at the sides to allow the devil within to leave their bodies in liquid form. If it made them laugh, then morale would remain high, well, for them anyway.

On the beach, a number of fires were started so alot of the rubbish could be burnt. Dale reminded us over and over again to ensure there was no ammo hidden in the mouldy tents or random boxes and crates. No one wanted to get blown up after the surrender, so we were thorough. We took abit of a breather, so our guys could dash off for a shit, and the prisoners could have a smoke. Beached next to the huge piles of ammo was a landing craft, like we had used to get into San Carlos. There were guys all over it putting the ammo onboard. Word got round that the engineers were going to take it out to sea, and throw it over the side, since there was far too much for it to be destroyed safely. I dreaded to think how much all that ammo cost, and all it was destined for was the sea bed. We were joined by teenage kids from Stanley who were walking around with big flasks, dishing out its contents to our lads. When it came to my turn, I found it was to be tea, very sweet tea, with enough sugar in it to make a fly diabetic. I wasn't going to complain, I savoured every moment of it. Our prisoners made themselves scarce and sat at the side of the road sharing a cigarette or two. Maybe after occupying these people for three months, I think they knew the chances of them getting a cup of tea were as good as zero. I noticed Zane accept a cup of tea, and take it straight over to the prisoners, who accepted it gratefully, after all, it was a bloody cold day, and weather reports indicated it wasn't going to get any warmer. Everyone stopped what they were doing to watch Zane's random act. This guy looked like an axe murderer at the best of times, but was now displaying random acts of kindness on more than one occasion. The teenagers looked at each other, shrugging shoulders, when one of the girls walked over to the prisoners and started dishing out the brew. Sheepishly, her friends followed her example. Some of the lads walked across the road and started giving out cigarettes. I felt a huge swelling of emotion brew up inside me, and I tried my hardest to keep it in, but my eyes gave it away. I caught the gaze of Leighton, who just nodded and winked at me, nothing more needed to be said. No one else needed to die here.

Zane came over to where we were standing. He lit himself a cigarette and looked out over the harbour, deep in thought. Davo piped up.

"Getting soft in your old age mate."

He blew out a mouthful of smoke and looked at the floor.

"They're just kids, not much older than him." With that he pointed at me.

Davo glanced at me, and then nodded in agreement. Alot of our prisoners were fucking young, fresh out of school if a day. I was young, but I was in a far better position than they were. Better trained in all our Platoon weapons. Better fed, though you wouldn't believe it by the look of me right at this moment. Better paid, my bank credits would be looking rather flush upon my return. Physically fitter, though the tab across this bloody island would lead you to believe otherwise. All in all, a better soldier than these poor sods sat at the roadside. Dale snapped us all out of it.

"Right you bunch of soft twats, before we start playing football in no man's land, get this fucking racecourse sorted, snap to it."

Flasks empty, the teenagers waved goodbye as we made our way back onto the racecourse, to finish up our tasks for today. It was looking a damn site better than it did yesterday morning, apart from the odd random clutter to be collected and burned. All that remained to be done was filling in holes and putting the turfs back. Our prisoners understood what needed to be done, since some of them knew basic English, and got on with the gardening. We huddled together, trying to keep warm, hoping the girls would come back with fresh flasks and warm smiles. We noticed Justin doing the rounds with our moaning gentleman from yesterday, inspecting all the positions where the guns were placed. He was making notes, which he would probably have to pass onto whoever deals with ruined racecourses. As he drew near, we could still hear this old twat rambling on about how we caused more damage towing the guns to the beach. Zane flicked his fag butt into one of the waterlogged holes right in front of the old fart, who looked up red faced, on the verge of rage. Zane glared right back at him. Justin rolled his eyes and gave Dale a look and a flick of the head in Zane's direction. Justin ushered Mr Angry to the next position, Dale came level with Zane and gave him a raised eyebrow. Zane capitulated.

"Fair enough, I'll behave."

Dale gave him a pat on the back.

"Chill out mate, let's just get this done and get the fuck out of here. Ungrateful bastards, the lot of em."

Situation defused, we went about keeping warm, and watching landscape gardening, Argentine style. After a while, the prisoners had done as much as they physically could with regards to sorting out the turfs on each gun position. It still looked a bloody mess, but that was about as good as it was going to get until people could come in with some serious machinery and resurface the whole damn racecourse. We allowed the prisoners one last cigarette before they made the long, cold trek back to the airport. As they wandered off, it quickly dawned on us that they didn't have an escort. No one appeared to give a toss, since I doubt very much these young exhausted lads were going to kick off now they had handed over all their weapons and ammo to us. We wandered back towards the bungalows in dribs and drabs, with not much else to do for the time being. The remainder of the Battalion, plus other units living in Stanley were dealing with tidying up their parts of town with their prisoner labour, so we didn't feel the need to volunteer our services, and sought the warmth of our accommodation.

As Jamie and I drew near our bungalow, I could hear shouting and the clattering of furniture. We turned the corner to see Phil and Dale in the midst of a full on domestic with another man who was throwing the stacked up shitty furniture all over the garden. If I was a betting man, I would guess this was the owner of the bungalow. He was having a right old wobbler. He insisted his furniture was put back in the house, right now. Dale informed him his men's health was a priority, not the ruined furniture. The owner then informed Dale that his men, meaning us were to clean it and get it under cover. Dale clench his teeth and his fists and told the irate owner that was not going to happen, and that he was to complain to whoever he needed to with regards to the Argentines vandalising his property. Jamie turned and looked at me with a rarely seen worried look on his face. Would Dale forget himself and his position and just wade into the civvy? Place your bets. The argument then turned onto the subject of who gave us permission to stay in his house. This was just getting better by the minute. I'm not an aggressive person at the best of times, but I now wanted Dale to lose his cool and smash this civvy prick all over the garden. Disappointingly, Dale was not taking the bait; he calmly informed this prick that he was to air his displeasure to the Brigade Liaison Officer who was stationed at Government House with Brigade Headquarters. With that the civvy stormed off, probably towards Brigade, and as he marched off he was ranting on about how we should hurry up and go home. What a wanker. Dale slowly turned on his heels slowly and found Justin stood on the porch, nursing a brew and a beaming smile. Dale vented.

"These fucking people."

Justin chuckled.

"I've made you a tea, Sergeant Major. I was worried you'd beat him up, but well done for not doing so."

Dale looked at the tea for a second, and then accepted it. Justin and Phil patted him on the shoulder, and went back inside. Dale took a sip, when suddenly his eyes narrowed to a glare.

"What are you pair of idiots looking at?"

He was talking to us. Jamie and I looked at each other for inspiration, caught bang to rights.

"Piss off before I feel the urge to have this furniture cleaned." He emphasised the piled up chairs with a kick. We skirted past him and went into the bungalow, trying not to laugh.

Personally, I'd pass the point of giving a shit already about these backward farming fuckwits. The Argies were more than welcome to the place, if this was what the people were like. We hadn't ventured any further into town as of yet, so hopefully, the two bell ends we'd met at this stage were a minority. The remainder of the evening passed without much going on apart from smoking, chatting, and listening to really long guitar instrumentals from a grown man in a school uniform. And before you ask, it wasn't one of the lads.

15

The following morning was a slow and lazy affair. We were not due to have our church service in town until late morning, so there was no need for a mad rush for the shaving queue. I lay in my bag just watching the world go by. The majority of the lads who had the shits yesterday had a bit of colour back in their cheeks, and were no back in the land of the living. Some of the early birds were up and dressed already, sorting out their bergens. Some smoked just outside the front door. The conversations were a random collection of subjects you would eavesdrop on in a pub; the due date of a baby, the price of a patio in Andover, their dickhead neighbours D.I.Y in the middle of the night, stuff like that. Jamie was still nothing more than a sleeping green maggot next to me. Word come round for the church service, only one magazine would be carried attached to rifles, but gimpy gunners would not have belts fitted, and was to leave all our kit at the bungalow. We were to be in berets and combats, nothing more. The majority of the room were still in bed, so I didn't feel the need to turf my arse out of bed any time soon. This theory was short lived when Dale walked in from outside and told us all to get up and get sorted. It took a brave man to ignore Dale when there was stuff he wanted doing. Green maggots soon came to life. Jamie sat up with the hood still up on his bag. The maggot spoke.

"You can do breakfast, I can't be arsed."

I clambered out of my bag, and slowly got dressed. Once shaved, and boots polished, I rummaged through mine and Jamie's bergen for food, and got to work out in the garden with cooking. Just to keep the cold off, I had the duvet jacket on, which still smelt abit ropey. Jamie joined me outside now dressed, looking not too sprightly.

"I had a terrible dream last night."

"Oh yeah" I asked, "what about?"

"I dreamt we had to get out of these houses and move back onto Longdon until it was time to get on the boat, and everything was frozen."

"Blimey, that's abit random."

It would be the start of a long spell of random, fucked up dreams for Jamie. Nothing to do with combat, just a random collection of images all thrown together, as he would put it. We ate breakfast with not much to chatter about. We were rather bored of sitting in Stanley already, and the worse bit about all of this was not knowing when we could go home. Breakfast finished we went about making sure our shit was sorted for the church service. When the time came, Dale called the Company out of their bungalows onto the road. We gathered on the road and got into three ranks and face down the road into Stanley, as if we're going to march onto a parade. Sergeants and above would form up at the rear of the Company. Dale then ordered us to walk casually down the road until he told us to stop, and then wait for the other companies in the Battalion to join us on the road. After abit of milling about, with everyone trying to be in charge, the Battalion was finally in three ranks ready to march to church. For those it applied to, rifles were to be tucked in under the right armpit, and gympy's were to be carried on the right shoulder. O.B then moved into a position where he could command the Battalion. He roared out the order for attention, and the Battalion slammed to attention. The locals who came out to line the street got abit of a fright. O.B then gave us the order to quick march, and the Battalion then set off, all in step into town. As we began to march, all the locals lining the street cheered and waved us on. It came as a relief, since the first couple we'd met had really got our backs up, and we pretty much tarnished them all with the same brush. I was so happy we were wrong. I felt myself swelling with pride, and I must admit I was enjoying this march to church. As the Battalion drew up alongside the church, O.B roared at us to halt, in which we crashed to a standstill. The Commanding Officer and other Officers were already waiting for us at the front of the church, chatting with the locals, plus the media. O.B ordered one rank at a time to file into the church, to reduce the gang fuck trying to get everyone in and seated. It took abit of time, but the entire Battalion, plus some locals and media managed to squeeze into this little church for our service.

The Battalion's Padre, Fran, was what you could confidently call one of the few conscripts in the British Army. A man of the cloth, let it be said, but vicars tend to be pressed into a couple of year's Military service, so they can be the spiritual anchor for young men who have to destroy fellow man as a profession. They assume the rank of Captain, just to add weight to their role in a unit, but they rarely throw their weight around with regards to what we call rock, paper, and rank. Fran was a scouser, I met him when I first joined the Battalion, since part of the induction into the unit, you have to attend 'Padre Hour', and just so you know you have an impartial shoulder to cry on if you feel the chain of command cannot help. Padre hour was a laugh. He would crack jokes, and even when he was trying to be serious, you'd roll up laughing because his strong scouse accent made it sound like stand up comedy. He was hard as woodpeckers lips, before he joined the church, he was a bouncer, and bare knuckle fighter, and had the scars on his face and knuckles to prove it. His tattoos were as good as any Para's let me tell you.

Fran asked for us to remove our berets, and then commenced with the service. He reflected on the entire campaign as a whole. San Carlos. The lunacy of the Argentine pilots. The horrible march east. He then was very detailed and sincere about Mount Longdon. Our casualties, our friends, our enemy. He then asked for a moment of silence as he read out the names of those that had fallen. Besides Fran reading out the names, you could hear a pin drop in that church. When he read out the names of Danny, Tony, Kyle, Brandon, John, I swallowed hard to avoid the lump in my throat, but my eyes welled up, and I could just about hold it together. I peered left and right of me, hard men were openly sobbing, sniffing heavily. Arms went around friends shoulders, backs were rubbed, and there was no shame in crying here. We had been through one hell of a time in the last few weeks, and the whole magnitude of what we had undertaken had now caught up with us. Once the names were read out, Fran stood silent, for reflection. His eyes were now glazed and bloodshot. One of his grim duties was to formally identify the soldier when his body was back loaded to Teal, prior to them going into the temporary grave. This was his Battalion, and his war, and his parish that were dead, dying and maimed on that cold, grim mountain.

After a short period of time, he asked us to replace our berets, and thanked us for coming. O.B then stood up the front and asked us to leave in an orderly fashion, but feel free to have a look around Stanley at our leisure, return to our Company lines when ready. This was, as far as wars were concerned, an afternoon off. We slowly moved outside, and there were small groups of lads wandering off in all directions. Jamie and I decided to wander further along the beach road just to have a look about. There were prisoners mooching about with brooms and black bin liners picking up random rubbish from the gutter, whilst their guards looked on.

Our Second Battalion had yet to have their church service and was cracking on with their clear up duties. We nodded to the guards, continued on our way. On the sea front, the wind had really picked up and really bit through my clothing. I had a shirt, woollen jersey and my smock on, but no duvet jacket. I felt it bad taste to wear it considering where we had just been, besides, I didn't want Dale or O.B catching me with it on, since that would be grief I just didn't need. As we walked past a gap in the bungalows, we noticed a huge trailer with what looked like four light grey crates on it. One of them had the end of it missing and the whole construction was angled upwards at nearly forty five degrees, less the trailer. What the hell was it? I peered in the open end of the long grey crate, and it appeared to be all scorched and burnt inside. The crate itself was made of a metal of some kind, and had French writing in a black font along all four of them. Jamie and I were none the wiser.

"I wouldn't prat around with that if I was you." said a voice.

We peered around the other side of it, and there stood a couple of Military Police.

Jamie stroked one of the cased ends of the crates.

"What is it?"

"Exocet", answered one of them, "anti-ship missile."

So that was the streak of light that we saw shoot out of Stanley that night.

"Fucking hell" I shook my head

French missiles in Argentine hands, I think a couple of high profile heads might roll for this one.

Jamie and I continued with our sightseeing. We just wandered down whatever street looked inviting, some of which were still ransacked with military kit all over the place. Down one particular street was a column of armoured cars, about ten of them. We walked around them with interest, thanking our lucky stars that these bad boys were not deployed as we moved in towards the racecourse. They looked brand new, probably taken off a ship, parked up here and forgotten about. Up and down the street, the locals just went about their business, some saying hello as they passed. In a children's playground next to the swings was one of the biggest artillery pieces I had ever seen. It wasn't ready for action, still in its stowed position. If they had got this beast into the fight, they could of really have given us a pasting on that mountain. If the Argentines were aware of what hardware they had in the town at their disposal, and had the cunning and know how to use it effectively, we could very well be sitting up in the mountains even now, freezing our arses off, running low on ammo, scary shit. Stanley wasn't the biggest town in the world, and it wasn't long before we'd seen pretty much all what it had to offer. Prisoners were clearing up their mess all over the town, all looking very miserable and bloody cold. We thought of taking a look at the airport, but I couldn't be arsed to go and look at a shot up airfield occupied by a miserable army. We slowly made our way back to the bungalow.

Back at the bungalow, most of the Platoon had already been back a while, and were in their usual positions. We got ourselves a brew on the go, when Davo walked in and called for everyone's attention.

"Listen up guys, I have some news you might be interested in."

He instantly had the Platoon's undivided attention.

"The O.C and Dale have flown to Teal for a small service for our boys. The prisoners will be shipped home on the Canberra, starting tomorrow."

If he was expecting cheers, it wasn't forthcoming, fuck them, when are we going home?

"Once the prisoners are out of here, we will hand in all our ammo and specialist kit to Phil, who will be getting it ready to freight on the Norland."

This was more like it.

"Once the ship is packed, we will board it along with the Second Battalion, and getting the fuck out of here."

There was a thunderous roar from the lads. This was sweet music to our ears. Getting the fuck out of here, going home, amazing. Almost straight away, AC/DC crashed into life; hairs on the back of my neck were stood on end. G.I's on their way home from Vietnam must have had this feeling flowing through them, knowing there was an end to their ordeal. Still floating on the good news, I went outside and savoured my brew in the cold sunshine. Some of the lads went about packing their bergens as if we were about to get on the boat right now. Almost like children on Christmas Eve, wishing tomorrow would hurry up. It would all come soon enough, and we could hopefully catch some of the British summer, which would be a damn sight warmer than this one. I went to bed that night, without a snowball's chance in hell of sleeping, since the room was just a beehive of conversation, and packing of personal gear.

Morning came, the same as the last couple. Piss, wash, shave, get dressed, tea, coffee, nicotine for those that required it, and the same bland breakfast. There was however, a very beautiful sight sat out in the harbour for us to look at whilst we ate. As I emerged from the bungalow, I could see some of the company gathered on the beach admiring the view. I strolled down to join them, and sure as shit, there she was, in all her white, rusty, and bullet holed glory, the Canberra. Landing craft were ferrying the first batches of prisoners from shore to ship, and slowly but surely, filling the boat. She was too big and sat too deep in the water to be able to moor up at the jetty, hence the landing craft. It would take a fucking age to fill her with the thousands of prisoners that were queuing from the jetty all the way back towards the airport. I don't think we complained too much, we just glad to see her. Fuck knows how long it would take for her to sail to Argentina, off load, and steam back. It didn't matter; we would soon be out of here. We milled about for the remainder of the day, with the Canberra slowly filling. Phil made the command decision to start receiving in the specialist equipment from the guys such as night sights, binoculars, compasses, even watches from those that had to be issued one, mainly Commanders. The ammo would be a mission for tomorrow. It took next to no time to gather all the kit required in off the guys, and we all lent Phil a hand getting his freight ready to go for loading onto the Norland, whenever she arrived. The loading of prisoners would last well into the night, but the view was just as marvellous, since all the ships lights were on, in the dark, she looked even bigger.

The following morning, the Canberra had set sail, and it appeared that the Argentine Army had as good as vanished. Stanley was a ghost town. Even the locals were treating themselves to a lie in. Word comes around for the Battalion to get its freight down to the jetty ready for the Norland's arrival. Second battalion would load theirs first, followed by us. Judging by the time it took us to load all our shit onto the Canberra in Southampton back in April, we knew there was no rush to get down there, so we could get all our ammo handed in and packed up. Phil instructed the company to get all their ammo down to the beach. Word come down from the Quartermaster of the Battalion than any ammo that had been broken out of its packaging would be gathered up and destroyed. Another small African nation's budget was about to become fish food. Apart from the crates of ammo we'd got off the Chinook a few days ago, nothing else could be salvaged. The guys, including me had unloaded our personal gear of all our ammo and had it piled up in front of us, and as Phil came down the line to scrutinise what could be saved, a very scary revelation became clear. Almost all of the company were in possession of Argentine ammunition.

Our ammo was one tracer with every three normal on a belt. The Argentines had a mixed bag of orange and green tracer on a belt of normal rounds. I only found out later that the green tracer was in fact Armour Piercing rounds, holy shit. It quickly became apparent that we had run out of our own ammo quicker than planned and had resorted to scrounging ammo from enemy positions, some food for thought maybe for the big planners of this whole bloody campaign. Once again, it was arranged for a landing craft and engineers to take this ammo away and feed the fish with it.

Early afternoon, the MV Norland made an appearance in the harbour. Second Battalion were on the jetty with all their freight ready to go, and the manpower to get in on in a short amount of time. We had begun to get our shit to the waterfront, with whatever was to hand. We had managed to scrounge captured trucks, tractors and trailers, you name it. Our company freight was pretty poxy compared to the likes of Support Company. They had Mortars, Machine Guns, and MILAN to get freighted onto the ship, and that took a shitload of muscle and sweat. B Company patiently waited its turn. The Battalions ammo that was still crated from San Carlos was a bastard of a job, and all hands to the pump were needed to get that cracked. It was almost dark when it was our turn to get our freight onboard, but when you know that the end is upon you, you don't mind busting a gut through the night. We returned to the bungalow in the early hours of the following morning, all giddy with excitement of our impending departure. I packed all that was not needed in the morning, so there was minimal fucking about. No one slept, we just sat around shooting the shit, smoking, laughing, drinking brews, all the usual carry on of troops just burning time. The early light of dawn had arrived, so we got our shit together, and moved it out of the bungalow into the garden. Davo spammed me with wiping down the kitchen and mopping the floor, wanting to leave the place in as good state as possible, despite the shitty furniture still stacked in the garden. Everyone mucked in getting the bungalow ship shape, and we closed the front door behind us. It was very cold outside, our breath very prominent in the cold air, but we didn't mind, it felt good for the first time in a while.

Dale shouted for us to get our gear on, and form up onto the road. I put my gear on with ease, since we no longer hand loads of ammo, water and rations rammed in it. Once the company had finished larking about, we managed to get into three ranks. Dale didn't bellow drill commands, he just told us to start walking. We knew where to go. The other companies were marching parallel to use in the next street. They were all smiles as well, and laughter could be heard until one of their seniors told them to keep the noise down. We arrived at the waterfront, and moved off the road. Without being told, most of the company were removing bergens, and sitting on them. Some stood and lit cigarettes. We just past the time of day once again, waiting to be called forward to board the ship. The Norland was half the size of the Canberra, and she was moored at the jetty, which suited us, no more bloody landing craft. It wasn't long before we received the order we had dreamed of for the last couple of days. We got to our feet and put our gear on. As B Company began to climb the gang plank, I got all emotional, and managed to get a grip of myself before I became a sobbing mess. With glazed eyes I looked up at the Norland, whose decks towered above me, and instantly I was overcome with the desire for a nice long hot shower, and a beer. The shower would come soon enough, my first in weeks.

As for the beer, that would have to officially wait until I was eighteen.

EPILOGUE

We arrived at RAF Mount Pleasant after a bloody long flight, nineteen hours. This didn't include the three hour refuel at Ascension Island. The DC 10 was on its regular shuttle from Brize Norton all the way down to East Falkland. Jamie leant across me and peered out of the window and nodded.

"Yep, same shite weather."

When we were allowed to leave the aircraft, we made our way down the steps and followed a member of the RAF movements control people into the terminal. Mount Pleasant wasn't exactly Heathrow, but it was a busy airport nonetheless. Whilst waiting for our baggage to be recovered from the plane, we had to listen to a mandatory briefing about minefield awareness. The place was still littered with the fuckers. We each got issued a map, highlighting the areas that were out of bounds, yet civilian organisations were working tirelessly searching the open moorland with a fine tooth comb for the little bastards. It was common for cattle to wander where they shouldn't, and the farmer would hear a loud thud as his prized Hereford would cripple itself. Once the brief was finished, our luggage was on the carousel, and it wasn't long before we claimed what was ours. Our guide for our visit was a rather attractive redheaded woman called Vicky, who ushered our group outside to a series of land rovers. We all clambered in and slowly made our way out of the airbase on route to Port Stanley. A solid hard standing road had long since been built connecting all the settlements to the capital.

Our party consisted of me, Jamie, Davo, and Phil. We were also accompanied by mine and Jamie's sons, Robert and Daniel respectively. Both Robert and Daniel were Corporals in our old Battalion, and were veterans of both Iraq and Afghanistan. My boy Robert was in B Company and Daniel was a member of Patrols, who still carried out the same tasks as they did thirty years ago. Without sounding bias, they were both good operators, and had the humility to ask their superiors if they were unsure of things. They both volunteered to come with us all the way here during their leave, since the Battalion was once again getting ready for Helmand

Province, and couldn't spare them at any other time, much to the dismay of their girlfriends. I had recently retired from the Army in the rank of Major; my last appointment in the Battalion was Quartermaster, which was not at all fun. The entire Battalion equipment list and budget on your shoulders. Be too lavish with the equipment and the money, you got your hand slapped by the Whitehall bean counters. Be too cautious, and the boys on the shop floor thought you was a career minded wanker, you couldn't win. In my free time, I would walk the dog, keep myself in pretty decent shape and just enjoy a handsome pension, and whatever hobbies I had going on at the time. I tried golf, but that was just too boring for me, I'd rather watch paint dry.

Jamie left the Army a few years before me, finishing his time with the Battalion as the Regimental Sergeant Major, who the hell let that clown be RSM wants their head seeing to. My best friend did a great job, all the way through our careers and lives we have been thick as thieves, and he just had enough at the end of his twenty two year career, and had the bottle to leave. He got involved with the security scene over in Iraq for a short time, but when he found out it was full of Walter Mitty clowns who talked a good gunfight, he told them to poke it up their arses and returned to the UK, and became a personal trainer. He now owns his own gym, and let's just say, he enjoys a very comfortable life.

Davo married Sam when he got back. They now live in Chichester, had a couple of kids that have now pissed off to University, still costing him a fortune. Davo left the Army as a Captain after serving as a Company Commander at our Recruit Depot. He now does adventure hikes and stuff with civilian clients paying him a fortune to take them up Snowdon and places like that. Sam works with him and squares away all his admin for him whilst he walks his party all over the hills. Not a bad living.

Phil, our old Company Quartermaster, is clearly the eldest in our party. He retired after a full career, and went onto be a Yeoman Warder of all things. Taking crazy tourists all around the Tower of London telling them all the grim stories in which they hang on his every word. Phil and his wife lived in apartments in the Tower, and I was invited to spend the weekends there on a number of occasions. Drinking in their exclusive bar was a nice experience, listening to all their stories of this and that, and not having to tell them the same stories over and over again when you first meet people and they find out you was in the Army.

The drive to Stanley took about forty minutes, and it wasn't long before the road took you around the base of Mount Harriet on our left side. Mount Harriet was one of the Commando objectives on the same night as ours. As we got closer to Stanley, Sapper Hill and Mount William could be clearly seen over to our left, with the Summit of Tumbledown further to the north. We entered the outskirts of Stanley and were stunned with how much it had grown. There was building projects all over the shop. A lot of money had really been poured into here. The islands enjoyed the wealth of tourism since the war, as people became inquisitive about these small islands in the South Atlantic. We drove down to the waterfront where the jetty was, and that brought out a few memories and we took the mick out of Phil for that bloody long day fucking around with the freight. He gave us the finger and just looked out the window, which made us roar even more. Back then we wouldn't have dared make fun of Phil, since he was our Colour Sergeant, and we were just two cheeky Private soldiers. Our guide pulled up outside our dwellings that would serve as home for the next few days, and we clambered out, grabbing our gear, and made our way inside.

Vicky introduced us to the lady of the house, and she was in her early forties maybe, so therefore just a child when we were here last. She gave us the grand tour and showed us to our rooms. Being typical soldiers, you never lose the habit; we literally slung our gear into our rooms and made our way back down to the little bar they had, and pitched up there for the rest of the evening. It was wonderful to be with my son and some old friends, chewing the fat, drinking beer, and putting the world to rights with regards to our old Battalion, the rights and wrongs of Iraq and Afghanistan, and all the usual shit pissed soldiers waffle on about when they've had too many beers. The lady of the house was great company, and didn't mind staying up with us while we put money behind her bar, and almost drunk the place dry. Our hangovers would not be forgiving in the morning.

What possessed me to drink that much last night is beyond me. Why do I do it? Like a dickhead, I had a hangover that would kill the average civilian, and had a long walk ahead of me today. I gingerly got out of bed and got myself sorted. I would not be wearing uniform for this one. I had decent walking boots and cargo trousers, with some decent warm clothing, and windproof jacket that is all the rage in the mountaineering community, plus my walking rucksack, which had some items that I needed to deliver whilst I was here. I made my way downstairs to breakfast, and took no prisoners on the menu. I ordered a full monty truckers special, with extra fried bread. I was going to need it today. One by one, the survivors of last night emerged and joined me at the table. Robert and Daniel were the last to appear, saying something about how the old and bold can put their drink away. I caught Phil's gaze and he just winked, which he then stated that the Battalion couldn't drink for shit these days, since they spent too much time in the gym, and worrying about looking pretty. This made Jamie and I chuckle, and our sons held up their hands in capitulation.

Once we'd eaten ourselves back into the land of the living, and drank our body weight in tea, our very enthusiastic guide arrived. She was mainly there to help Phil, since we'd elected to walk, but Phil's tabbing days were long over and he and the sexy redhead were going to meet us at the top. We got our gear together, and made our way outside. Phil and Vicky clambered into the rover and made their way out of town. We began our trek at a gentle stroll, the weather forecast was set to be good for this time of year, it would remain cold, but nothing we couldn't handle. We kept to the road that hand railed the beach. We came across the South Atlantic Memorial which we took time to look at and read. We then continued on, to where our bungalow was situated. It was still there, the garden had a makeover, but other than that it was still as it was, just with a new lick of paint. No one was in, but a neighbour called out of their window stating that the owners were back in the UK visiting family. We thanked them for the information and pressed on. We were on the road that would lead us to Moody Brook and the base of Wireless Ridge. On our left side around the racecourse, was a load of new buildings that was something to do with a Cable and Wireless Company. We eventually arrived at the old barracks site. It had long been ripped down, and was now a cluster of official looking buildings. I remember watching some of our lads searching a couple of prisoners here, then giving them a cigarette and sending them on their way.

We began our ascent of Wireless Ridge, luckily the three of us old bastards were still in semi-decent shape, with Rob and Dan streaking off and waiting for us at the top fresh as daisies. So they bloody well should, they were serving members of the Parachute Regiment, something seriously wrong if they were lagging behind us. We got to the top and caught our breath before we made our way over to the memorial that was for our Second Battalion. It was a large silver cross, with numerous wreaths around the base of it. Three names were engraved there, the guys they lost on that night. It caused me to reflect. This was meant to be one of our objectives, and these guys had already done their bit at Goose Green, such a shame. I took off my rucksack and reached into it. I fished out a large bottle of single malt and placed it next to the guy's plaque. No one said a word, it wasn't needed. I got my gear back on, and turned around. There it was.

I remember even as a Sergeant Major having to attend a veteran's lunch at the old Airborne Forces Museum in Aldershot. It was located in the old barracks that was once our Recruit Depot. That place was nothing more than a compound of misery and suffering for me as a recruit, and as a Sergeant Major on that particular day, I was overwhelmed with butterflies and dread, that's how much I detested that place. Career wise I almost shot myself in the foot when I refused to go there as an instructor, where it would be me dishing out the torment, I just couldn't bring myself to go there. The same could be said in this case. From where I was stood, Longdon looked like a sleeping dinosaur with us stood on its tail. The plan was to meet Phil and Vicky at the site of our RAP, and from there climb up to the memorial as a group. We began our ascent of Longdon, at a casual pace, since I was keen to have a real good nose around. We came off the high ground of Wireless onto the shallow saddle that separated the two features, and we began to climb up onto A Company's position at the end of the battle, known as Full Back. The cover they would have had during the shelling appeared rather sparse, we definitely had the better cover that day. They were on a forward slope in full view of Stanley and the enemy gun line on the racecourse, not ideal at all. We inspected their bunkers. Those with overhead protection had through time and bad weather partially collapsed revealing the contents within. Rotten sleeping bags, a mouldy kit bag with some clothing spilling out of it, empty bullet cases, old ration tins well faded over the years. Some of the old trenches we found had no cover, and were now overgrown with heath grass and ferns.

In the centre of A Company's position was the remnants of a flak gun, it's chassis all rusted and buckled out of shape, and around it was the random debris of equipment we couldn't recognise. I stood behind it and noticed it had a fantastic arc of fire all the way up to our position on Fly Half. Was this the nemesis that kept 4 Platoon pinned in the alleys? The history books would have you believe it was naval gunfire that knocked it out, but after a number of chats with members of Support Company on the way home, they claimed the crew was obliterated my machine gun fire, and the weapon knocked out by MILAN. I didn't see what happened that night, so this claim will remain out with the jury. We slowly made our way up to Fly Half, it became apparent how open the top of Longdon was, and would be plain suicide for anyone to want to occupy the top, since it was a forward facing slope towards Stanley, and dominated by Tumbledown to the south. Hence why the Battalion hunkered down on the north side, throughout our time on the objective. Over to our left side was the infamous anti tank gun that knocked out one of our support teams. It now faced Tumbledown which I found rather bizarre. Why would anyone move it? As we climbed up onto Fly Half we found evidence of where the fire support teams had once been. Spent cases and machine gun link all over the place, plus rusty broken ammo tins were littered everywhere. Those teams were truly exposed that night, with just darkness as cover; it took some guts to remain in that position for all of that time.

We moved over to our right and came to the lip of the bowl. How different it looked after three decades. Some of the bunkers could be seen, the rest were overgrown with ferns and heath grass. We carefully clambered over the lip and down into it. Amongst the ferns we would trip on an empty twisted ammo tin and find the odd rifle magazine rusted beyond use. We inspected a couple the bunkers, pretty much the same contents as encountered on Full Back, the grim corpses and vile smell had long gone. We made our way down to the bottom of the bowl and moved around to the left. Phil and Vicky's rover came into view marking the old RAP site; Vicky knew this spot well, since this is where she would start the Longdon battlefield tour for the tourists, which I found rather bizarre. I never would have classed Mount Longdon as a site for tourism, but the general public have a morbid fascination for human conflict, me included. As we drew close to the vehicle they both got out. Phil got himself ready for the short sharp climb to the top. Vicky suggested she remained with the vehicle, since she wisely felt her knowledge of the battle wasn't required today. We thanked her for her understanding and arranged to meet her in a couple of hours back here.

Once sorted, we set off. We left the RAP and made our way along towards our old Start Line. We kept to Phil's pace and every now and again we would stop to recollect what was happening at this place and at a certain point in time. Back then, when I was freezing cold, and fucking scared did I ever imagine myself walking the battlefield with friends going over the events of that awful night, all that time ago. We began to skirt around to our left and climb up towards the alleys. It looked so much more of a placid place this time around, not the grim, deadly objective that chewed up 4 Platoon that night. Because Phil was not as young as he once was, we didn't climb up through the alleys to get back to the summit, we continued to skirt around to where our Platoon had to fight its way up. Rob and Dan were truly fascinated with the whole experience. They also added into the experience a modern day view of how they felt the Battalion would have dealt with this objective. We all stood facing our old Start Line, with Jamie as our Patrols expert showing us the route he would have taken us if he was guiding us in, and to be fair he wasn't far off the actual route we took.

We turned and faced up on to 5 Platoons objective, the route up to Fly Half. A real maze of rock, long heath grass and ferns. The wooden beams of a few of the positions that had overhead cover could be seen, but time and weather had perished alot of the bunker features. I took this opportunity to show Rob and Dan the bunker I fell into, its wooden supports badly rotted, and the hole was waterlogged. My boy put a hand on my shoulder, thanking me for winning the brawl that night, and gave me a hug, the silly sod. We began to pick our way up through the rocks and long grass, inspecting the bunkers as we went. It wasn't long before we found Danny's bunker. It was no less John's or Brandon's, don't get me wrong, but I always referred to it as Danny's. As Davo, Jamie and I explained what happened here, our boys shook their heads and let out a low whistle. It was at this point Phil apologised for not being with the Company that night, and got abit silly and emotional. In all honesty, it wasn't his job, his job was to get ammo, rations and water forward, and he'd passed any fighting appointments in his career by that point. He composed himself, and apologised once again for being silly old sod.

We climbed up onto Fly Half, and made our way over to the left where the Battalion memorial stood. As with Wireless Ridge, there stood a large silver cross, and at its base was a large collection of plaques dedicated to the Battalion, plus plaques dedicated to individuals by both family and friends who had recently made the long pilgrimage here. We took our time reading them, reflecting on every name that was engraved. I removed my rucksack, and carefully placed it at my feet, and unzipped the main compartment. Carefully, I removed a small wreath, which was dedicated to the Battalion by Dale's widow. Dale had lost his long struggle with cancer just last year, and had never returned to Longdon. Dale was regarded as a legend amongst the old B Company boys, and across the Battalion as a whole. We all missed him. He acted more like your dad than the Company Sergeant Major, which kept the boys in line on more than one occasion; he was without a doubt a true role model of mine. All the way through my career, I just wanted to do right by him, and do things his way, and it bloody worked. I missed him.

I placed the wreath at the base of the cross, and dug into the rucksack once again. I pulled out a large bottle of single malt for the boys, placing that next to the wreath. Davo had found the large ammo tin, which had a visitor's book in it. The book was in a thick, clear plastic bag for obvious reasons. We all added our thoughts and messages of respect into the book, and ensured the book was well wrapped up back in the tin for the next visitors. I had one more gift to deliver. I pulled from the rucksack the duvet jacket Jamie had got for me in the RAP. It had been laundered a thousand times since, and was my chosen piece of warm kit throughout my career. It had given me an element of kudos all the way through my career. I was that bloke who had a dead Argentine's jacket, whether I was in barracks, or away on a career course. The jacket was the topic of conversation. I lost count how many times Rob had asked for it, but I refused to let him have it. I place the jacket at the base of the memorial and found a large enough rock to hold it in place so it wouldn't blow away.

I didn't need it anymore.

Mount Longdon

This name broke the hearts of many mothers on that awful night.
Thirty five years ago.
Their sons are listed here.

JUAN DOMINGO BALDINI
VICTOR RODRIGUEZ
IAN MCKAY
ALFREDO GATTINI
DARIO ROLANDO RIOS
IAN SCRIVENS
TONY GREENWOOD
GUILLERMO GRANADO
PEDRO ALBERTO OROZCO
DONATO GRAMISCI
TIMOTHY   JENKINS
JOSE LUIS DEL HIERRO
MARCELO MASSAD
GERALD BULL
SCOTTY WILSON
ISSAC ERASMO ROCHA
JOSE LUIS RODRIGUEZ
OMAR ANIBAL BRITO
STEVE HOPE
MACEDONIO RODRIGUEZ
RICARDO HERRERA
DAVID SCOTT
STUART MCLAUGHLIN
MIGUEL ARRASCAETA
PEDRO VOSKOVIC
JAMES MURDOCH
STEWART LAING
NESTOR GONZALEZ
CARLO A HORNOS

RICHARD ABSOLON
PHILIP WEST
MIGUEL GONZALEZ
MANUEL A ZELARAYAN
CHRIS LOVETT
PETER HIGGS
JULIO HECTOR MAIDANA
ALEJANDRO VARGAS
CRAIG JONES
PETER HEDICKER
LUIS ALBERTO DIAZ
ROLANDO PACHOLCZUK
ALEX SHAW
NEIL GROSE
DANTE LUIS PEREYRA
MANUEL JUAREZ
JASON BURT
KEITH MCCARTHY
ANGEL BENITEZ
RAMON QUINTANA
ENRIQUE RONCONI
MARK DODSWORTH
ALBERTO PETRUCELLI
MIGUEL FALCON
MIGUEL ANGEL PASCUAL
JOHN CROW
JULIO ROMERO
SERGIO CARBALLIDO
ELBIO EDUARDO ARAUJO

ALL WARS ARE CIVIL WARS, BECAUSE ALL MEN ARE BROTHERS

- Francois Fenelon

Printed in Great Britain
by Amazon